THE CETACEAN MESSAGES

cosmic wisdom from beyond

STEFFEN PATRICK

Planet Ocean Publishing

An Imprint of Planet Ocean LLC

PlanetOcean.com

Published by *Planet Ocean Publishing*
Email: publications@planetocean.com
Author Website: SteffenPatrick.com
Email: TCM@steffenpatrick.com

DISCLAIMER: This is a work of visionary fiction. While inspired by philosophical, spiritual, and experiential traditions, it is offered for inspirational and educational purposes only. The author makes no representations or warranties as to the applicability of the content and disclaims liability from its use. The truths and perspectives herein are offered freely for reflection and discernment.

Cover design by Simon Thompson
Interior design by Steffen Patrick

ISBN: 979-8-9916037-0-6 paperback
ISBN: 979-8-9916037-1-3 eBook
Library of Congress Control Number: 2025920960

Printed in the United States of America
Las Vegas, NV
First Edition, 2025

Table of Contents

Chapter 1

Encounter

Peering through my mask, floating face down on the glass-calm waters of Kealakekua Bay, I barely noticed the soft whistle of breath through my snorkel as the late-morning Hawaiian sun warmed my back. Twenty feet below the ivory sand reflected the sun's dancing rays as if set to an aquatic symphony of audible crackles and pops.

The ocean is anything but silent. A trained ear catches the constant chatter—shrimp snapping, parrotfish munching, waves lapping, triggerfish grunting, dolphins clicking, and whales singing. It's these latter two wonders that drew me out, alone, to this spot in the middle of the bay that gloriously sunny morning. Not that I really had any expectations of interacting, mind you. I was drawn mostly by the peacefulness that I experience being one with the ocean. Away from people and the "normal" sounds of the world, this aquatic sanctuary provides for me a calm not unlike what meditation might offer the yogi.

Steadily, I kicked away from the shore. The sandy bottom soon gave way to coral and rock formations, and then, finally, to a ledge that plunged over a hundred feet into the depths. Skimming over the abyss, I exhaled slowly, fully, to allow for a very deep breath. As I inhaled, I kicked myself forward, bent at the waist, swung my legs upward and began my descent—headfirst, into an ocean so blue it defined the very essence of the color.

Beneath me the bottom appeared like a ghostly mirage as I hovered mid-water, about forty feet deep. I'm always amazed at how clear this water is, and how far I can see. A hundred feet of visibility is the norm, and a very good day can produce twice that much. This was, indeed, a very good day.

The secret to freediving is slow, graceful movement. Amateurs rush their descent, only to run out of breath and bolt back to the surface within seconds. Experienced divers know that speed is unimportant. It's not how fast you go, it's how efficient you move. The objective is to conserve energy so the body will use less oxygen. Some divers even slow their heart rate, allowing them to achieve superhuman depths and times before resurfacing. I've measured my own pulse at depth—it drops to about two thirds my normal resting state. I get so relaxed, I instinctively feel like I'm floating in the womb.

Of course, with diving comes ear pressure—ask anyone who's sunk to the bottom of a deep pool. That pain? It's water pressure pushing on the eardrum. To avoid it, divers "clear" their ears—equalizing internal pressure with the water outside. Swallowing, or a quick nose-pinch-and-snort, usually does the trick—repeat often on descent… unless you're fond of ruptured eardrums.

Hanging weightlessly in translucent blue, I reveled in the underwater symphony and scanned the far reaches of visibility for the dolphin pod I knew was nearby. Their high-pitched squeals and clicks confirmed their presence. I could hear them all around me, even though I couldn't see a single one.

I drifted upward, eyes scanning the edges of visibility for a flicker of two-toned gray.

The strange thing about sound underwater? It's everywhere. Completely omnidirectional. You just can't tell where it's coming from. It travels faster—much faster—and farther than in air, making it nearly impossible for human ears to pinpoint direction. A dolphin's squeal could be a hundred feet away… or a hundred yards. It might be to my right, my left, above, below—or right behind me, like a mischievous prankster, keeping perfect pace behind my head as I spin, searching in all the wrong directions.

The truth is, no one gets close to a dolphin unless they allow it. By the time I spot one, it's already pinged me. It knows exactly where I am—and where I'm looking.

They're sleek, sentient torpedoes with built-in sonar and a sixth sense for fun. I'm just a clunky land mammal in flippers, playing in *their* aquarium.

Back on the surface I scanned above water for the elusive pod. Many times before I had been in this spot, and on several occasions I've been lucky enough to briefly swim alongside. But my encounters were rare. These particular dolphins that reside in Kealakekua Bay are shy, tending to avoid swimmers and snorkelers.

Hawaiian Spinners, they are called—members of the order *Cetacean* which also includes whales and porpoises—known for their enthusiastic jumping and spinning antics when surfing the wake of a boat or just playing away the day. They always look like they are having so much fun. As I saw a pair frolicking in the distance I daydreamed, *"When I die, I want to come back as a dolphin."*

I lowered my face back into the water and prepared to dive again. Instantly, a piercing message blasted through my consciousness, shattering my reverie.

It wasn't sound. Not exactly. I wasn't hearing it with my ears—it was more like a megaphone blasting from within. A statement. A question. A jolt—as if I was sensing it with some previously unused receptor buried deep inside the inner recesses of my brain.

"YOU CAN HEAR ME?!"

"WHAT?" I shouted back, raising my head from the water. It came out more like expressed confusion than as a question. I felt as if another entity had merged with my consciousness.

"You CAN! …you can hear me!"

This time, before I could answer, I was overwhelmed with... I guess I would call it... messages?

"Don't talk. Too slow. THINK... I'll understand."

This is seriously unreal, I thought. *I have to be imagining this.*

I scanned the water for someone, something, *anything* that might be the source of this unexplained voice. I knew I shouldn't be out here alone—but I'm a professional dive instructor. Surely the *'don't dive alone'* rule doesn't apply to me, right?

I reasoned there was no real danger. The tourists I escort aren't exactly rescue-qualified—in fact, they're usually just liabilities. If I got into trouble, they'd be witnesses at best. So what good would a buddy actually do?

I just hoped I wasn't cracking up. Drowning? That's a known risk. But spontaneous insanity? That's a new one.

I distinctly remember saying aloud through my snorkel, *"This is way, way too weird."*

I kept rambling to myself... *Had my eccentric hobby finally pushed me over the edge? Was I losing it?* The clarity and resonance of the message was inexplicable. It was more than sound... It seemed like pure *feeling!*

I took a deep breath and dove again, wondering if the voice would return.

Everything was peaceful—until a streak of gray shot by me so close I felt its wake, but not a touch.

Always before, if the dolphin were interested, they would slowly approach and maintain a discreet distance. Not this one. It was... different—behaving in a way I'd never before experienced. A blur of muscle, speed, and grace. I marveled at how well these life forms have mastered their aquatic environment. I was entranced and confused—so much so I almost forgot to surface and breathe... almost!

After a gulp of fresh air, I dove again—utterly fascinated. The strange alien "voice" from before had vanished from my mind. I was simply mesmerized by this incredible animal's grace and speed.

As I hovered at depth, the dolphin streaked to within five feet of me—a more comfortable distance. Then it began circling, clockwise, slowly—about five seconds per loop. I felt like the hub of a wheel as we rotated in perfect sync, our eyes locked. We weren't just looking at each other—we were connecting.

And then, the voice returned.

"I'm happy you can hear me. Your fear is killing us."

The tone was whimsical, almost cheerful—completely out of step with the gravity of the words, like a cosmic joke delivered with unnerving affection.

"Whose fear? Killing who?" I thought, not exactly sure if I was responding or just thinking to myself.

The answers came as fast as I could form the questions.

"Human fear. Almost everything. We are talking."

"What are you?" ...stupid question.

"I'm a dolphin, of course."

"Who are you?" That's what I meant to say.

"Call me Deja."

It was a she.

"How are you communicating with me?"

"Tediously. Humans aren't exactly the fastest communicators on the planet. You've yet to conquer the word barrier."

What I was receiving felt like pictures, feelings, and concepts all compressed together. My brain scrambled to translate them into words. But it was fast—blazing fast.

"Why are you... 'talking' to me?" It wasn't quite the right word, but I didn't have a better one.

"Now that's a better question."

I felt her playful humor—and a trace of impatience.

"You're receptive. You're available. And someone must get this message."

"What message?"

"Your fear is killing us."

"Mine? Who's 'us'"?

"Human fear. It's destroying everything."

Her words were dire, but the tone felt oddly gentle—wrapped in warmth and spoken with radiant calm. It was eerily disorienting.

"Killing dolphins?"

"Yes. Dolphins, humans, the planet. Your fear has outlived its purpose—grown to decimating proportions. It obstructs your ability to believe, trust, love... and it fuels your preoccupation with materialism. Your fear is killing us."

I stared, dumbfounded. Her warning was apocalyptic, but delivered with joy. Her apparent happiness made the message even harder to grasp.

"Why are you telling me this?"

"I already told you. You're available. You're receptive. And someone must get this message."

"Why me, specifically?"

"You are human, aren't you?"

"Of course."

"Your inability to recognize interconnection is part of the problem. When I say 'you,' I mean humanity. And your fear is killing us."

I understood—at least, partially. The "us" she referred to wasn't just dolphins. It was life itself. All of it. Even the planet. My intuition caught that—and she confirmed it.

"All life forms, including yours, are in danger of regression or extinction unless humans change drastically. It's time to reassess what you call 'important.' Your fear no longer serves you.

"Have I said it simply enough for you to understand?"

I still didn't. My mind was spinning. A conversation that should've taken minutes had collapsed into mere seconds—and I was bombarded not just by words, but feelings. So many feelings: peace, elation, sadness, joy, fear, love, urgency, awe.

Sensing my overwhelm, she softened:

"I see I'm going too fast. I'll slow down. It's rare for humans to perceive us at all. Most are unreceptive—stuck in a phase of suspended development. A few can grasp basic thought transfer. It takes effort on my end. Most just experience a "good feeling" around us—they're picking up on our natural exuberance. But overall, humans are tediously slow communicators."

"Should I feel insulted?"

"You may, if you like. But remember: dolphins evolved millions of years before you. That's a pretty big head start."

I was still processing when she added:

***"Okay… I'll slow w-a-**a-a-y** down*—like we're two humans talking. Honestly, it's like tutoring a very slow child."*

"Now I do feel insulted."

"Your feelings are part of the problem. You're ruled by them—constantly trying to alter your state. But don't take it personally. At least you're receptive. That's rare. If your ego needs it, take it as a compliment.

"It'll be a while before you regain thought transfer ability…"

Her sentence drifted off. Like she'd said too much.

"Wait—what do you mean 'regain?'"

She didn't answer.

"Remember, when I speak of 'you,' I mean all humans. You are inseparable from one another—and interconnected with everything, including what lies far beyond your current awareness."

Before I could respond, she swam away.

Frantically, I reached out—mentally broadcasting: *"Come back… I have more to ask. We're not done. I don't understand!"*

But she was gone.

Suddenly, almost in a panic, it hit me—*I needed to breathe.*

I hadn't surfaced during the entire exchange. Not once.

That's **impossible.**

Urgency rocketed me upward—exploding through the surface, gasping for air.

How long had I been under? Five minutes? Ten? More?

Normally, I'm tapped out at two. Three on a good day, with focus and prep. But this? This wasn't natural. It was *off the charts.*

Then again, so is talking to a dolphin.

I took several deep breaths, scanning the surface for her.

Nothing.

I dove again. And again. Hovering in the silent blue, I waited—hoping she would return.

But the sea was empty. Only silence.

Only blue.

Not even the ghostly seafloor—just infinite water, and the faint squeals and clicks of dolphins in the distance.

Running on fumes, and wondering *"what the hell just happened,"* I turned toward Napo'opo'o beach and slowly kicked back to shore.

Chapter 2

Total Recall

In 1981, Napoʻopoʻo is a quiet, time-forgotten place nestled in the southeastern curve of Kealakekua Bay on the Big Island of Hawaii. The tiny hamlet was once a thriving village, home to ancient Hawaiian rulers and the center of activity on the Kona Coast.

Captain James Cook landed here in 1779—credited with "discovering" the islands, though I think the Polynesians beat him to it by about a thousand years. He was also killed here. A 27-foot-tall obelisk marks the spot on the other side of the bay.

There are no hotels or condos. Only a quaint scattering of homes, most of them Hawaiian rustic and a few that are semi-palatial.

The population of about 75 is mostly local Hawaiians, with a sprinkling of eccentric "haoles"—Caucasians, as recorded by whatever U.S. bureau keeps track of such things.

Far from the resorts and condos, it's quiet and picturesque—an ideal hideaway for artists and fishermen. No shops, no restaurants—just a tiny lei stand run by a sweet local lady we call Nana, Hawaiian for grandmother.

The bumpy paved road is narrow; cars pull over when passing as unhurried neighbors always do. The tropical vegetation is lush, with ancient lava rock walls draped in night blooming cirrus. Swaying coconut palms are scattered throughout, especially along the waterfront where gentle waves caress the lava rock coastline.

An old concrete pier anchors the center of the village. A white sand beach flanks one side, with a black sand beach on the other.

The latter is where I came ashore and began sauntering back to my beach shack about a hundred yards down the road; past the park and the grassy basketball court, past ole Rob Wesley's house and across the overgrown lawn of wild grass leading to my humble abode by the bay.

As I rolled aside the heavy barn-style screen door and stepped inside, I still hadn't decided if my encounter with Deja really happened. I couldn't imagine telling anyone. What would they even say? No doubt they'd think I'd lost it.

Yet *somehow* I remembered **everything**—every feeling, every "word," the setting, and especially Deja's message in full.

I have a good memory, but never like this. I don't usually recall conversations word for word. But, strangely, I had retained this entire encounter—clearly, exactly as I experienced it—as if it had been imprinted directly into my brain. The degree to which I could recall the event was uncanny. When I closed my eyes, I found myself reliving it... including the feeling of ocean water against my skin—so much so, I had to open my eyes to make sure I was really dry and home instead of wet and forty feet deep.

My mind was flooded with questions. Why did Deja single me out? Then again... maybe she didn't. Maybe she tells everyone who ventures into the bay. If so, then why had I not encountered her before. After all, I've snorkeled out there dozens of times. For gosh sakes, I *work* underwater on the other side of the bay. She never contacted me there. So why today? Why me?

The questions kept coming: What exactly did she mean by **Your fear is killing us?** Humans have been fearful since the beginning of time, haven't we? ...and it's not like there isn't plenty to be afraid of.

"Heck," I muttered, "without fear we'd all been eaten by beasts or smitten by enemies long ago."

Seems to me that fear is a sensible reaction to a variety of circumstances... necessary to our survival... so why would she say *our fear is killing us?*

And what about her reference to thought transfer? Deja suggested humans once had it, but now it's suspended.

That didn't make sense. If our ancestors could do that, how could they just lose it? Wouldn't that be like forgetting how to read? ...or worse, forgetting how to talk.

More than anything, I wanted to know what Deja expected me to do with all this—if there even was something to be done. Surely she had more in mind than just, *"someone must get this message."* Now that I had it... what in heaven's name was I supposed to do?

Who am I—a dive guide on a tourist boat—to change the course of humanity's oldest instinct?

As I closed my eyes, I felt comfortably wet, forty feet deep, and fully adrift in the mystery of the day.

Finally, with the taste of salt water still on my lips, I surrendered to sleep—uncertain, awestruck... and hoping I hadn't imagined her.

Chapter 3

Circling The Bay

The alarm clock sounded at 7 a.m. Lazily, I got up, ambled downstairs, stepped out the garden door, and headed straight to my backyard shower.

Mounted to a green catchment tank, it was one of my beach shack's best features—simple, old-school, and perfect. The round, flat showerhead looked like something off a 1950s farm: no spray settings, just a full-volume waterfall from above.

I love outdoor showers. No steamed-up mirrors. And best of all? Showering in the rain. Hot water mixing with a warm tropical downpour—pure bliss. The best shower I've ever had... and so low-tech.

But this morning, I didn't have time to linger. It was a workday, and I had to stay on schedule.

Five minutes to shower

Five minutes to dress

Ten minutes to eat

Then out the door by 7:25.

Destination: Keauhou Bay, to work on the sailboat *Fair Wind*—which, fittingly, sails right back to Kealakekua Bay—aka **K-Bay**.

I always found that amusing: I'd leave K-Bay from Napo'opo'o, drive four miles up a winding road with ninety-seven curves to 1,200 feet elevation, cross nine miles of dormant volcano, then descend to Keauhou Bay—only to sail seven miles south by boat right back to where I started. Almost.

We moored the Fair Wind on the northeastern curve of K-Bay at Ka'awaloa, near the Captain Cook Monument—close enough that I could see my shack looking south across the bay.

So yeah. I lived on one side of the crescent-shaped bay and worked on the other… which meant, quite literally, that my life revolved around Kealakekua Bay.

As I sauntered up to the check-in window, I asked Julie, the office manager, about the schedule. She told me I had two divers—both certified.

Perfect.

That meant I could head straight to the boat and set up the scuba gear. I liked dive days best. They spared me from mundane chores—fueling the boat, prepping lunch, loading supplies, scrubbing the glass-bottom windows—and let me do what I loved: dive.

My role on the boat always depended on the passengers. If we had certified divers, I guided them—dream job. Diving was something I'd happily do for free. If not, I worked as crew.

Some days I took out experienced divers like today—people who'd completed a scuba course and were (hopefully) competent. Other days, I taught "Intros"—short for Introductory Divers—which meant giving a crash course on the ride to K-Bay. Intros were more work, but their wide-eyed joy always made it worth it.

Today, though, would be a cruise.

Set up the gear.

Brief the divers.

Show them the underwater wonders of K-Bay's marine sanctuary.

I'd help the crew here and there, but for the most part, I was off the hook.

Great, I thought.

As I attached the regulators to their tanks, my mind wandered. I wondered if I might see *Deja* again. After all, our dive site is barely a half-mile from where we'd met—well within the home range of the dolphin pod.

Funny, I thought. I've been diving this spot for over a year, and nothing remotely like yesterday has ever happened.

Wouldn't it be something if I had witnesses to…?

My thoughts were interrupted by a tall girl with frizzy, sun-bleached hair wearing a fluorescent orange one-piece bathing suit.

"Hey, lucky you today—two certs, yeah?" she said, referring to the certified divers.

It was Deb, my best friend and hānai sister. In Hawaii, it's common to informally adopt close friends as family—*hānai* means brother, sister, son, daughter, and so on. It's not blood, but it's close.

We often told guests aboard the *Fair Wind* that we were "brother and sister" who "had different parents together" and "went to different schools together." We usually finished the bit with, "Mom always did like you best"…a charade the passengers loved once they realized we were joking.

Deb had just stepped aboard, her smile beaming as usual, carrying a basket of buns, burgers, and all the fixings for lunch. This girl was the highlight of my life. I often thought I should marry her. But then the perks of being a 29-year-old bachelor would override my sentimentality, and I always concluded that it would only spoil a beautiful friendship.

"Yep" I teased. "Means I won't have to do any *real* work today."

"That's what you think, buster... guess what we get to do if there's no afternoon charter?"

"What... get off early?"

"Clean the engine room, that's what." She was still smiling. I couldn't understand how anyone could smile about a date with grease.

"Nah... say it ain't so"

"True story... Captain Liz is turning Capt'n Bligh on us. Says it's gotta git done."

"I *hate* cleaning the engine room. Besides, the customers never see it, so what's the point?"

"Eeez cuz we git one Coast Gawd inspekshun," she replied in mock pidgin—the unofficial local dialect. We weren't born here, but we'd spent enough time around locals to pick up the basics, and we bantered in it regularly—always in jest.

"Oh...? When?"

"Ah dunno, sometime next week I tink... whaz da matter you, ...you no like clean da- kine?"

(*Da kine*—Hawaiian slang for whatever you're talking about when you're too lazy to remember the right word. Think: *thingamajig*. But more specific.)

"I'd rather cut onions."

Deb laughed out loud. She knew how much I hate onions. She once caught me slicing them while wearing full snorkel gear to avoid the tear-triggering fumes. After which she'd threatened me with 'onion punishments' whenever I was 'bad.'

Our constant ribbing made working together a joy.

"Well, I guess you'd better pray for an afternoon charter," she said. Besides, tomorrow is my day off and you know what that's means?"

She looked up from unpacking the food basket and gave me a shit-eating grin.

"Yeah, ...means if we do it tomorrow, you get out of it. I hate when that happens."

She just kept smiling as she stored the soda and beer cans behind the bar.

"So, uh... Deb, did you happen to dive yesterday?" I asked casually, trying to sound nonchalant. Really, I was wondering if she experienced anything ...unusual.

"Yeah, had one guy—certified. He was a pretty good too. Piece of cake. Saw Orville and Wilbur and went down to the sand at hundred feet. No offense, but I kinda like it when yer gone—I get to take the divers," she laughed.

Orville and Wilbur were our two "pet" moray eels. Orville was about five feet long and looked ferocious. He was a regular at our mooring spot in K-Bay, and we always warned divers about him before each dive. Not because he was dangerous—actually, quite the opposite. He was so tame that he'd rush out to greet you. But, to the uninitiated, a large, friendly eel six inches away from your face can be quite unnerving—mouth opening and closing, exposing a jagged row of sharp, vicious looking teeth.

This was Orville's way of asking if you had any treats for him. The danger came from a diver freaking out—bolting to the surface or spitting out their regulator. In reality, Orville was like a big ol' underwater Saint Bernard. We hand-fed him and stroked him under the chin, on top of the head... everywhere. It was clear he enjoyed both the food and the petting.

He always made a great show, and we played it up like lion tamers at a circus.

Wilbur was Orville's smaller brother—a little shorter, not quite as fat, and almost as friendly. When they were both "home" at the same time, it was quite a thrill—and one we never got tired of.

"So... did you see any dolphin yesterday?" I asked, trying to keep it casual.

"Ahh, the usual. Jumping and spinning in the middle of the bay. We didn't really have time to make a pass through them with the boat. We were running a little late and we wanted to do some whale watching on the way back... didn't see any though. So, what'd you do on your day off anyway?"

"Well, actually I went snorkeling... on the other side of the bay" I hesitated. Should I tell Deb about Deja?

She laughed. "A busman's holiday, eh? Don't you ever get tired of being wet?" She was teasing, of course. We both loved the ocean and everything in it.

"Looks like it's time to go to work." Deb said, gesturing toward Captain Liz who was leading the passengers toward the boat, smiling and carrying her usual cup of coffee. It looked like we had about 30 people—a nice group for a boat that can hold fifty and still seem spacious.

Deb and I hurried over to the port side of the stern to assist boarding. Once everyone was aboard, Liz fired up the engines. Kristy, our fourth crew, tended the stern line while I untied the bow. Within seconds we were on our way to K-Bay for whale watching, a little trolling, snorkeling, diving, lunch, and unlimited fun in the sun.

✳✳✳

Three and a half hours later while cruising back from the morning trip, Liz called down from the bridge.

"Sixteen—no divers!"

Deb and I looked at each other, then shouted in unison, "YES!"

We had an afternoon charter—which meant no engine room cleaning duty today.

"So, who wants the afternoon off?" Liz continued.

It was 12:30, and we'd just gotten back into radio range. With only 16 passengers scheduled, we'd only need three crew. One of us could go home.

Kristy raised her hand and, since both Deb and I needed the hours—rent was due, and work had been slow—we agreed she could take it.

"So, Deb," I beamed, knowing how envious she would be. "I swam with a dolphin yesterday."

Her eyes lit up and her ever-present smile widened.

"You did?" she gasped, tugging on my arm. "For real? Why didn't you tell me?!"

"I just did."

Truthfully, I'd been aching to tell her all day—but I wasn't sure I hadn't imagined it myself. "I was gonna say something this morning, but we got busy and I forgot."

Total lie. I was still deciding how much to share.

"Oh wow, so... how come you nevah tell me nawting?" she teased in mock pidgin.

I decided not to go into detail. "Cuz, I no like make you jealous, az why" I teased back.

"Was it wonderful? How long did he stay with you?"

"It was a she."

"Yeah right! Like you can tell the difference," she said, grinning. "Com'on tell me more!"

I told her how a dolphin had rocketed past me within inches, then circled me slowly when I dove back down. But I stopped there. I couldn't bring myself to tell her that we'd actually talked.

Deb was fascinated... and definitely jealous.

"You think she was being aggressive? Maybe protecting keikis?" (Keiki is Hawaiian for child)

"No... somehow I don't think so. But I can tell you—it was the highlight of my day." *Understatement of the year*, I thought.

"Yeah, I'll bet ...did you tell Liz? ...Come to think of it, I *am* jealous."

"Nope, haven't told her yet... so, what, you want me to make her jealous too?"

"Yeah, I think you should," she grinned, as she turned to serve a customer at the bar. "Why don't you do the supply count, and I'll get the bar, ok?"

"Got it."

I started making a list of what we would need for the afternoon charter while Deb bounced between pouring drinks and glancing at me with an "I'm-so-jealous-I-could-just-spit" grin.

I wanted to tell her the full story but I couldn't. I knew she would just roll her eyes and think I was joking. Besides, some part of me was still trying to decide if it had really happened.

Secretly, I was hoping I wouldn't be needed at work tomorrow. If there were no divers, and a light passenger count, I might get the day off.

All I could think about was going snorkeling alone in the bay. Would I see Deja again?

I couldn't wait to try.

Chapter 4

The Trouble with Fear

Seven a.m. couldn't come soon enough. I woke just minutes before the alarm, anticipating its ring, and went straight for the phone. I had to know if I would be needed to work on the *Fair Wind*. It was Tuesday and although I was on the schedule, I also knew that only 20 people had signed up by closing time yesterday—and none of them were divers. Unless the count had increased, there was a good chance I could get the day off.

Two rings. Answering machine.

"Damn," I muttered. Nobody there yet.

Julie was usually a few minutes late. I figured I'd shower, then try again.

Towel in hand, I stepped outside, turned on the shower and immersed myself. A couple of mynah birds were squawking over a freshly fallen papaya a few feet away. They scattered when they noticed me watching.

I spotted another ripe one still hanging with breakfast written all over it. *Looks like they left one for me*, I thought.

I rinsed quickly and called again. This time, Julie answered.

"Do you need me today?" I asked. No small talk—this was routine. She knew my voice and expected the call.

"Well, let me see... I just walked in and haven't checked the recording yet. Give me five minutes and call back."

Damn, I thought again, but agreed.

The suspense was killing me, but I stayed on schedule—just in case.

"Breakfast," I told myself.

My kitchen was in the tiny backyard cottage—technically Glen's place. The property had two structures: my beach shack and Glen's one-room cottage. The owner rented them together, so when I found the place, I offered Glen the cottage if he agreed to share the kitchen. My shack didn't have one. Letting him take the kitchen meant I'd have more privacy—and fewer bugs. Kitchens in the tropics tend to attract things with too many legs.

I grabbed the papaya on the way in. Glen was still in bed.

"You working today?" he mumbled, barely awake.

Glen was a local boy—happy-go-lucky, a diver, and part-time captain on the *Fair Wind.* He was also a good friend.

"Dunno yet," I said. "Julie told me to call back in five. Can I use your phone?"

"Sure," he snorted, rolling back under the covers.

The cottage was basically a studio, no divider between bed and kitchen. I always felt a little weird cooking while he was sleeping, but he never complained. The rent was cheap, the location unbeatable—and he knew the kitchen deal up front.

I called again.

"Julie, it's me. What's the scoop?"

"Looks like we don't need you," she replied. "Twenty-seven, no divers. Liz, Kristy, and Tom can handle."

"Great!" I was elated. Normally this news would disappoint me, but not today.

"What about the afternoon?" I asked.

"Only three signed up so far."

We needed at least sixteen for the boat to go out.

"So, you want me to call in later or...?"

"Nah, I doubt we'll go. If we do, we'll send Frank. If there's any divers, Tom can handle it."

"Thanks, Julie. I'll check in later about tomorrow. See ya."

By now, Glen was sitting up in bed and my eggs were crispy on the bottom and sunny side hard in the pan. I'd forgotten they were cooking.

"Sounds like you don't want to work—I thought you needed the hours."

He was smiling his toothy grin and looking at me as if he'd just seen a starving man cheerfully refuse a piece of chocolate cake. It was true. At $4.50 an hour, the only way to make ends meet was to work nonstop. Fortunately, I loved the job. I didn't even *call* it work. Glen knew all that and I'm sure that's why he was surprised.

"Yeah... well, I've, uh, got some other stuff to do today." I felt like a kid caught ditching school. No way could I tell him I was planning to go talk to a dolphin. He would no-doubt think I was crazy. I also knew that, unless he left today, it would be hard to hide the fact that I'd gone to the bay to go snorkeling—which, of course, I could have gotten *paid* to do if I had worked.

He didn't pry. Just smiled knowingly, figuring I had a hot date with one of the babes I met on the boat. He just put on his shorts and bounced into the kitchen to fix his own breakfast.

"What are you doing today?" I asked, hoping he wasn't sticking around.

"I told Peter I'd help him rebuild his engine," he said, cracking eggs and popping down the toaster. "I hope he's pulled it out already... don't want to hurt my back again lifting anything heavy."

I offered him the other half of my papaya which he gladly accepted. We chatted a few minutes longer before I excused myself and headed back to my shack. I had my answer. Now all I had to do was get to the water.

With a quick glance over my shoulder, I grabbed my mask, snorkel, and fins, then headed down the partially paved road to Napo'opo'o's black sand beach.

✳✳✳

It was still early, only about 8am. The sun was up but the tall cliff bordering the bay was casting a morning shadow over the water near shore. Normally, I'd wait until the sun rose fully above the rim—light always makes the underwater world brighter. But today, I was too excited to wait another hour.

By the time I kicked out to where I'd first met Deja, I felt a little foolish. I doubted she would return. I couldn't help thinking that maybe I'd imagined the whole thing. After all, everything we "said" happened during a single breath-hold dive.

I kept telling myself, *That's impossible*—but the memory remained crystal clear. Every word. Every feeling. It had to have happened.

At the edge of the submerged slope, I dove to about thirty feet. Just as I leveled off, I heard a tender voice:

"Of course it happened... I'm surprised you doubt reality so easily."

It was Deja. I couldn't see her at first, but within seconds she was circling me again.

"Why did you leave so abruptly last time? Why did you come today?"

She ignored my first question and answered my second.

"I returned because you are still confused ...isn't there more you wish to know?"

"Thank goodness," I thought. I was more than confused... I was borderline distressed—not just about my sanity, but from the onslaught of *why's* and *what's* that hadn't let up since the last encounter.

Deja continued in that same tender tone, *"You're still uncertain about the connection between your fear... and how it's killing us, aren't you?"*

"Well, ...yeah. I guess I am."

This time, her communication felt slower—more like casual conversation. The emotional barrage was dialed down, too. I could sense that Deja had softened the vibe, making it easier for me to absorb what she was about to say.

I ventured a guess, trying to relate what I knew. *"Isn't fear one of our most basic instincts? A survival tool that's helped us evolve?"*

"Yes. Without it, the human species wouldn't have lasted long enough to develop minds capable of asking questions like that. Your earliest ancestors were driven by raw instinct—deeply fearful, for good reason. But that animal legacy now runs unchecked. What once protected you now mutates into things like jealousy, greed, and hatred—distorted echoes of the original instinct. And these distortions are what keep you from fulfilling your destiny… a destiny you were designed to achieve from the very beginning."

I couldn't help thinking the obvious: *"What exactly is our destiny? And who designed us?"*

Somehow, Deja made it clear I wasn't ready for that answer—yet. Oddly, that made me happy. It meant there was more to come—more lessons, more visits, more time to see the larger picture.

I remember thinking, *"this is getting cosmic"* …and Deja trivializing my thought with what seemed to be a dolphin snicker.

Slowly she approached and offered me her dorsal fin. As I reached out to grab hold, she gently blew bubbles from her blowhole—reminding me it was time to breathe. *What a reversal this is*, I thought, sipping air like someone drinking from a water fountain as she continued.

"Humans have always been afraid. In the beginning, it was physical pain—hunger, thirst, injury. Rational fears. But then imagination got involved. Suddenly, lightning meant the gods were angry. Famine meant they were displeased. You began explaining the unknown with stories—and the stories got bigger than the facts."

She let that linger before adding:

"Ironically, those fears led you to seek understanding. Even to seek your Creator. So in that way, fear served you. But unbridled, it metastasizes like a cancer—spreading jealousy, greed, hate—the very things you claim to despise. These are the fears that are killing you."

"Okay, so give me an example."

Deja didn't answer with words. She answered with images—flooding me with a harrowing rush of vivid, graphic scenarios:

Vicious cycles of suspicion-based hate, fueled by jealousy and greed. Hardened walls of separatism, nationalism, and language barriers. Overpopulation straining already fragile systems. Misunderstandings deepened by calculated deceptions. Unabashed materialism powering the engines of exploitation. Power brokers tightening their grip while vulnerable minorities struggle to survive. All of it accelerating—a mounting momentum of conflict, with Earth's harmony teetering on the edge of calamity... poised to unceremoniously end the marathon, absent of heroes or champions.

"Oh geez, thanks for the visual." I felt myself trembling, utterly shocked by the brutal clarity of it all.

"Does it really have to be like that?"

"Of course not," she replied cheerfully. *"That's just the path you're on. Remember, your future isn't written. You're not stuck—you're steering."*

She sounded almost amused.

"I thought a reality check might inspire your interest to look at alternatives."

Still stunned, I nodded slowly.

"I'm not sure if you're ready to hear this, but we need to start somewhere. So, let's begin... with **death.***"*

"Death?" I was incredulous. *"Isn't death more of an ending than a beginning? I mean... if we're trying to solve the planet's problems, I really don't see how starting with* **death** *is going to help."*

Maybe Deja was right. I wasn't ready for this.

"Isn't death your greatest fear?" she asked gently.

"Hell yeah!" I shot back. *"I'd say 'fear of dying' pretty much tops the list."*

"Good, I like to start big and work my way down."

"Deja, don't you think fearing death is... reasonable?"

"Not really. Not anymore. Maybe once—back when your survival as a species depended on it. But now, with billions of you on the planet? I'd say it's time to shift the focus. You have a saying, don't you? 'Quality over quantity'?"

"Uh, yeah…"

"Try applying that to living as a species. You'll find the improvements worthwhile."

*"But how can anyone **not** be afraid of dying?"* I was exasperated.

"By knowing that physical death is only a temporal illusion."

Her words landed like a thunderclap.

My mind went silent for several long moments. I am not a religious person. True, I was sent to church for a few years as a kid, but I noticed my parents usually stayed home. Their absence was more memorable than any of the sermons. "God" seemed like something "religious" people believed in. And death seemed to be as life-terminating as it appeared... the final stop at the end of the line. Kaput.

Deja was right about one thing—I was **not** ready to believe her *opinions* about death. And I most certainly wasn't ready to stop being afraid of it.

*"You have forgotten that you are **spirit** having a human experience,"* she said softly.

Again, I was reminded that *you*, meant *all of us*.

*"In your quest to understand the universe—your origins, your meaning, your Maker—you found science, and it brought clarity. Yet by embracing only what could be measured, you dismissed what could be **felt**. Spiritual insight was sidelined.*

"Yes, your tools have evolved—but your instincts remain. Fear still rules you. It clouds your judgement and it sabotages your future."

As Deja glided us slowly forward, I held on—periodically catching a breath from the bubbles she released, captivated by her flow of thoughts.

"All who believe that physical death is the end of life shall not be disappointed—it is, for them. Only by knowing the journey continues, can you pass through the portal of death with personality intact—thus beginning the next leg of your spiritual adventure.

"For those with faith, death is not a concern. It's simply nature's way of discarding a body that's done its job—freeing the embryonic spirit to grow and journey onward, no longer bound by planetary limits."

I streamlined my body to make our glide more fluid, listening skeptically as she continued.

"Okay, even though you don't believe in life after death," Deja added, sensing my doubt with a trace of playfulness, *"just for fun—**imagine your spirit on a fresh new adventure, having shed the physical body that's no longer needed.***

"You've awakened in a new realm—free of pain, free of fear. Your spirit is pure energy—curious and alive—having entered a dimension of indescribable grandeur, brimming with infinite potentials.

Where you once strived to understand a small planet, you are now surveying a universe—filled with personalities you recognize and others that are dawning to meet you. You are fresh again—novel, bright and loved. Although untested in your fascinating new world, you welcome the challenges—armed with the exhilarating knowledge that faith is your passport on a journey toward completeness that you'll savor for all eternity."

It felt like a passage from a sacred hymn. But then, Deja abruptly severed the vision:

"Or if you prefer, you can choose death as an ending... both are available."

I woke instantly from the sweetest of all vivid dreams—and simultaneously learned the meaning of hell. Not fire and torment, but unconsciousness forever. The extinguishing of personality. The soul that, for lack of faith, chooses not to continue. Not damnation—just silence. Eternal sleep. No joy, no adventure, no next chapter. No triumphant return to the source of all creation.

Deja's alternative threw open a window to spiritual reality. It suddenly felt obvious—so obvious I was embarrassed not to have seen it sooner. *I am spirit—having a human experience.* That truth lit me up. For one dizzying moment, I felt free—my fear dissolving, replaced by something far better: **faith**.

"That's how it works," Deja said.

But then my logical mind snapped back, reclaiming its throne. Although what I was *feeling* made her case compelling, I couldn't quite accept that something as elusive as faith could be the antidote to fear.

Before I could form the objection clearly in my mind, she answered it.

"Faith is the golden key to the doors of trust and love. It's essential for gaining a longer-term perspective on life. After all, Heaven isn't a place—it's a journey. And that's a good thing, because eternity's a long time… and it would be awful to get bored along the way."

My rational brain scrambled for reasons to reject it—but even as it tried, it recognized the futility of using a worldly mind to explain that which is not of this world. And I almost laughed aloud when it hit me: everything about this entire episode was equally inexplicable.

I mean, here I was, gliding underwater on the back of a dolphin while discussing the nature of existence. Yeah, right. She was feeding me air from her blowhole, somehow maintaining the perfect speed so my dive mask stayed in place instead of being ripped off by water resistance.

None of this should be happening.

"Are all dolphins this well-versed on the workings of the universe?" I wondered.

"Is this really even a dolphin?"

Deja heard me, of course—but offered no answer. Just silence. She seemed to be enjoying our peaceful glide. Then suddenly, we surfaced.

Quickly I realized, *"Oh, time to breathe."* Before I could react, I heard a sharp *"whoosh"* from her blowhole, followed by a crisp sucking sound a split moment before she dove again—so fast I had no time to inhale for myself.

Before I could panic, a trail of bubbles came streaming toward me, reminding me that Deja could breathe for both of us. I pursed my lips to filter the air and repeatedly cleared my ears as we descended again.

"Why did she choose death as the first fear for me to face?"

Deja finally broke her silence, *"Unless fear of death is put into perspective, other fear-based problems remain unsolvable."*

"For instance?"

"Greed—a manifestation of a variety of fears. Fear of scarcity; fear of failure, fear of being left behind. The fear that if you don't take it, someone else will."

"But aren't those sometimes... reasonable fears?"

"They can be. If your survival is truly threatened, that's not greed—it's rational response. But hoarding or consuming far beyond your needs? That's greed. A failure to trust the abundance of the universe. A disconnection from the deeper truths of spiritual existence."

She paused to let that settle. Her rhythm was always patient—like a teacher who already knows the ending but lets the student discover it.

"Can you see how your view of survival influences your behavior?"

Even though she was starting to make sense, all I could think of was, *"Yeah, but..."*

Before I could fully form the thought, Deja countered.

"If you believe this life is all there is, then—why not consume it all? But that short-sightedness leads to crises that eventually require cures more destructive than the original problems."

In my mind's eye, I saw it: *disease, famine, war*—although she didn't *say* it. After allowing the meaning of that vision to sink in, she continued.

*"Once you understand that your personality exists beyond physical death, doesn't it redefine what **is** and **is not** a rational fear?"*

It was a stretch for me, intellectually. But emotionally? I felt it. Day-to-day worries shrank when viewed through the lens of eternity.

She let the silence stretch... then delivered a line that shocked me to the core.

"In case you haven't noticed, human greed is responsible for depleting your planet's resources and driving the greatest mass extinction since the age of dinosaurs."

There was a brief shift in her tone—just a flicker of intensity. And somehow I knew she wasn't exaggerating. Later I learned she was right—science confirmed we've entered an unprecedented wave of species extinction, fueled by habitat destruction and unrelenting human expansion.

Regaining her tender demeanor, she continued, *"Too many of you are stuck in the belief that life on this planet is all there is."*

I felt her words settle into my bones.

"Your decisions are based on a tragically short-term perspective. You pay only lip-service to your planet's well-being, and give almost no thought to a spiritual future.

"Overpopulation is looming, but you keep seeking ways to grow. Rain forests are shrinking, yet you lack the will to stop the destruction. Oceans are being depleted, yet you refuse to make the sacrifices that would sustain their bounty. You know these facts—and still you fail to act."

Her tone was almost lyrical, but the urgency cut through me like a blade.

"Even your compassion," she added, *"often lacks wisdom. Short-term fixes undermine long-term sustainability, because you refuse to look beyond this lifetime. Your fear of making hard choices is poisoning your future."*

I let that sink in.

"So you're saying our greed for living now is threatening our ability to live in the future?"

"Precisely," she joyfully replied. *"Spiritually, physically, and generationally. Your greed for the moment is endangering all that lives—and all that might live— on this planet."*

Abruptly, Deja slipped my grip and rocketed laterally into the blue. Confused, I looked around and realized we'd drifted far from the reef. Beneath us, the water dropped into open ocean—visibility stretched nearly 200 feet, but I saw no bottom.

A cold knot of fear tightened in my chest as I followed her gaze. A ten-foot Oceanic White-tip shark had noticed us.

Although Oceanics are sleek and magnificent animals, they're also one of the few potentially dangerous types of sharks—right up there with Makos, Tigers, and Great Whites. If given a chance, they can be man-eaters, and they deserve an abundance of respect when encountered in open ocean.

Normally, sharks won't bother healthy dolphins—but at our slow pace, we could've been an easy target for an Oceanic lucky enough to catch us off guard. I was grateful for Deja's alertness. The shark could've had us for lunch. Like most predators, he was looking for an easy meal—but Deja's sharp, aggressive response convinced him to look elsewhere.

Having repelled the threat, she hastily returned, once again offering me her dorsal fin along with a generous stream of steady bubbles, which I badly needed. My noticeably pounding heart had seriously depleted my oxygen. It took several deep breaths, and a few minutes, for me to calm down—and I used that time to silently flood her with gratitude.

Although she never acknowledged it, and acted as though nothing unusual had happened, I could tell we were heading back toward shore by the change in the position of the sun.

"Many of you fear that your life is an accident of chance," she said, *"that your adventure ends when your body dies. That fear—that belief 'you only go around once'—is what drives you to consume everything in sight."*

I hesitated to disagree, then I disagreed. *"Deja, not everyone feels that way. Not everybody fears death, you know."*

I felt kind of hypocritical as I said it, having just experienced how much death still scared me.

"Isn't that a bit harsh? I mean, not everyone is like that. I think you're making a big generalization, don't you?"

"Of course I am!" Her demeanor changed to feigned indignation... pretending she was insulted.

*"That's how teaching works. One must generalize when describing **patterns**. Quibblers dwell on exceptions. Yes, a shaky foundation doesn't always bring a house*

down. *Two monkeys with damaged DNA might still produce a genius. An atomic bomb might leave one building intact. But wise architects will still say faulty foundations are dangerous. Scientists won't breed broken monkeys. And nearly everyone agrees: atom bombs destroy everything."*

Her tone softened again.

"It is indeed comforting that many among you live spiritually, keep fear in perspective, show wisdom in your compassion, lack greed, and seek long-term solutions. This lends great hope for your future. Together, you can accomplish far more than you realize. Ten men can lift a great load—but only if they all lift together at the very same moment. A thousand men are of little more value than one if they fail to coordinate their efforts."

She paused for me to absorb her thoughts.

"The reality is, those who are enlightened have yet to reverse the momentum of materialism. Your population is still growing. Your resources are diminishing. Extinctions are accelerating. It doesn't have to stay this way. In fact, there is great hope—even expectations—that coordinated efforts will soon alter these trends for the better. The irony is, despite your problems, you now possess an excellent opportunity for improving the human condition.

"With wisdom as your compass, compassion as your guide, and patience leading the way—anchored in faith—you'll find no better moment than now to take giant strides toward the destiny you were designed to fulfill.

"That is why we are talking."

Then, without warning, Deja slipped from my grip again, banking gracefully away like a silver jet. As her sleek form faded into the deep blue, a final message rang out, clear and unmistakable:

"Advancement, in a spiritual being, can be measured by the absence of irrational fear—the scaffold upon which your human survival once depended. That scaffold has outlived its purpose. It now encumbers you. Replace it with faith—nurtured by love and compassion—as you prepare to step into the next epoch of human evolution."

I floated to the surface. Her departing words echoing through me like a sacred chord. Breaking softly into sunlight and fresh air, I was relieved to see I was just a few yards from the reef where she and I first met.

For a long moment, I lingered—suspended in the ocean's gentle rhythm, soaking in the distant chorus of ordinary dolphin sounds: rapid-fire clicks, playful chirps—beautiful, but wordless.

Eventually, I snorkeled slowly back to shore, the world above water both the same and somehow irreversibly changed. I felt lighter, freer— as if a layer of fear had dissolved, and I was becoming new again.

Chapter 5

The Clock of Time

Ooooooouuuunnnnk! The conch shell bellowed over the din of excited snorkelers—splashing, laughing, squealing, and sharing fish stories.

"All right, everybody, last call for lunch."

Deb, conch-blower extraordinaire and queen of the mic, grinned while waiting for the punchline to land.

"What...? Last call? What happened to first call?" some passengers called out, confused.

It was a daily jest aboard the *Fair Wind.* We loved it because the guests always stopped what they were doing, suddenly worried they were about to miss lunch.

Feigning confusion, Deb asked, "What, you haven't eaten yet?"

She paused just long enough, waiting straight-faced for the crowd to get the joke.

"Na, na, na, just kidding," she chortled, before launching into her animated spiel.

"OK, everybody, this is it. *First* call for lunch! Now, the way we work lunch is—you start over here on the left-hand side of the boat and grab yer buns," she paused theatrically—then continued, "the whole wheat kind, that is. Then work yer way 'round the bar as you load up on all the fixin's. Don't forget the fresh-cut pineapple, and be sure to try our famous Kona potato chips. Tell whoever's behind the bar what you want to drink, and we'll be happy to get it for you. And, when you get to the end, go see Capt'n Liz at the grill—she'll have a cheeseburger waitin' for ya. Any special requests—no cheese, medium rare, still mooing," she laughed, pausing for effect, "let Liz know, and she'll cook it however ya like."

"Oh yeah, don't be last in line, 'cause today we have 39 people and only 38 burgers," she lowered the mic and chuckled, "...and the rule out here on the *Fair Wind* is, *'you snooze, you lose.'* "

Another joke we used to get everyone to eat at the same time. Funny thing though—some people believed it. They'd take us aside and quietly offer to skip the burger if it meant someone else wouldn't get one. Truth was, we always packed extra—and a few guests would even get seconds. We loved to keep the mood light. Our jokes let them know we weren't just working, we were having as much fun as they were.

The art of running this kind of tour operation depends on the crew's ability to stay on schedule without looking like we're trying to. Passengers often said it felt like they were *out on a private boat with a bunch of friends*. We took care of everything professionally, but casually—all the while looking like we're having the time of our lives.

Deb continued, "By the way, we still have about an hour left before we cruise outta here to head back home, so you'll have plenty of time to go back snorkeling after you've finished lunch. And, if you've got any leftover burger or bun, toss 'em to the fish and watch out for the feeding frenzy." She glanced at me and winked. "But, be sure to throw everything else in the trash... the fish don't much like pineapple, chips, cups, napkins, plates... stuff ly'dat."

By now, the guests were swarming the bar like trigger fish on a tossed burger bun. Deb joined Kristy to help with lunch. I'd just returned to the boat after escorting my two Intro divers—was busy storing tanks and answering fish-questions when the conch blew.

Back to the surface world, Cindy, one of my Intros, picked up right where she'd left off before the lunch announcement.

"What was that funny yellowish fish that looked like a blob on the coral?"

"A frogfish," I responded as I stacked the last tank on the rack. "Also called an anglerfish."

"Well, I just had no idea what you were pointin' at 'til I saw the critter move," she exclaimed, her spicy Southern accent wrapping around every word.

Her husband Bart chimed in, "Yeah, I thought it was just another chunk of coral. I kept trying to figure out, *what the heck is this guy so excited about?*' as you were pointing at it."

Classic honeymoon energy—he was from California; she sounded like Louisiana. He'd talked her into scuba diving, and she'd only agreed to please him. But now? She was hooked—and was actually the better diver.

No surprise. Nervous and unsure, she clung to every word of the lesson, following instructions to the letter. Bart, on the other hand, was all swagger—probably sat through the briefing just to humor her. Underwater, he burned through his air like wildfire, flailing like a rookie. She moved with calm precision, barely using half a tank.

"They're called anglerfish," I continued, "because the first spine on their dorsal fin has evolved to mimic a tiny 'fishing pole' with a fleshy lure on the tip."

I wiggled my finger above my forehead to demonstrate. "They perch motionless, dangling the bait just above their mouth. When a smaller fish comes in for a closer look—BAM—they suck it in. It happens so fast it looks like the fish just vanishes. It's one of the fastest strikes in the animal kingdom."

They both stared at me, wide-eyed.

"Yeah... I really thought it was just a rock or somethin'," Cindy said, shaking her head. "I just couldn't believe it when I saw it move.

Then I noticed the eye, and I thought, *'Oh Lord... that's a fish!'* I just never imagined anything like that before."

"Hey, you guys are missing lunch," I shifted gears politely so I could go help the girls. They always gave me a hard time for chatting too long with my divers while *they* were doing the work.

"Better go for it while it's happenin'. Can I buy you guys a beer or something?" It was customary to offer the divers a drink after a dive.

"Sure," Bart replied.

"Oh, no thank you," Cindy replied. "I'll just have a Coke or something."

"Cool. Drinks are on me. Pick 'em up at the bar. If you'll excuse me, I'm gonna help the girls. It was great diving with y'all, and we can talk more after lunch."

Cindy smiled at my weak Southern drawl as I headed toward the bar to relieve Kristy.

"Oh wow, 'bout time you showed up." Deb teased me. "Tought you wuz going talk-story fo' days!" —which loosely translates to: *I thought you'd never stop bullshitting with those people.*

"Ah, you're just jealous cuz I got to dive while you had to work," I shot back.

"Not!" she grinned, handing out sodas and refilling the chip bowl. "See that cute guy over there?"

I glanced toward the bow. Tan, muscular, early thirties, sandy hair under a white visor—one of the tour escorts with that Midwest group of fourteen.

"Mark?" I guessed, trying to remember his name.

"Yeah, cute, huh? He asked me out for a drink tonight." She grinned, "I played hard to get..."—pausing to flutter her eyes dramatically and sweep her curly blonde hair off her neck—"for about ten seconds. Sooo, what-da-ya-tink? Wuz I too easy?"

"Wow, Deb, ten seconds? I'm shocked he didn't give up" I was ribbing her, of course. "Now tell me—are you asking for my permission, my approval, or just trying to make me jealous?"

"Make you jealous, duh," she playfully smirked as she pulled out a piece of fresh fish she had marinating in the cooler. Deb didn't usually eat burgers. After five years on a boat that served them daily, I couldn't blame her. I still liked them—but I was only a year into the job.

"And what a great job—diving in paradise, fun in the sun, cheeseburgers for lunch, and girls in bikinis. Sometimes I even got lucky."

Of course, for Deb, it was guys in shorts. No matter. We loved each other like siblings—no strings, pure fun. We both enjoyed the perks of our job, and occasionally played wingman for each other. It was all part of the times and the lifestyle.

"Tell you what—I'll tend bar on the way back while you flirt. Consider it payback for showing up late to lunch."

"Mm-hmm, I think that's the *least* you can do," she beamed mischievously. "Ya know, Patrick, you are so wonderful... sometimes... for a guy, ...no, really."

She was teasing, and I loved her for it.

Finally, the food line passed, and it was the crew's turn to eat. Liz leaned in over the back bar.

"Toasted buns?" she asked.

"Yep. Double my cheese," I called, tossing her a pair.

Diving always made me hungry. Today was no exception.

"So, Deb, have you ever spent any time with the dolphins in the water?"

It was almost noon. We'd just finished eating and were cleaning up from lunch. Some passengers were on the top deck working on their tans, while the rest were back in the water snorkeling.

"Well, here and there, I suppose," she said. "I mean, I've seen them underwater, but they don't stick around... nothing like what you told me you saw a few of weeks ago."

It had been twelve days since then—ten since I last saw Deja. I'd been on the boat every day since, secretly hoping she'd visit while I was diving with guests. She had to know I was there. Half a mile was nothing to a dolphin, and that's all that separated our rendezvous point from the *Fair Wind's* day-mooring in the bay.

What I really wanted were witnesses. Someone—anyone—who could verify my story. I was dying to tell Deb the whole truth, but the fear of sounding crazy had me biting my tongue. I couldn't chance being labeled a wacko.

Deb probed, "So... have you seen any more since then?"

"I'm sure I would have told you if I had."

I lied—knowing in that moment I might never find the courage to tell her.

A small part of me had been hoping, maybe, she'd had a similar experience. I knew it was a long shot, but I was desperate for some shared thread of understanding. Without that, I couldn't bring myself to open up.

Truth be told, I was scared.

Scared she'd think I'd lost it.

Scared I'd lose my best friend.

The idea of people labeling me as the 'dolphin guy,' isolating me from the friendships I'd worked so hard to build, terrified me more than I cared to admit.

As we headed back to port, as promised, I manned the bar while Deb made points with her new admirer. Kristy worked on her tan, and Liz drove the boat. Normally, Deb and I would improv a two-person comedy act for the guests. Sometimes I'd relieve Liz at the wheel for a bit.

But today, I was content behind the bar—cutting pineapple, pouring drinks, trading jokes with passengers.

Yet a part of me was miles away.

Even as I wiped down the counter, my mind kept drifting back to *Deja*. Her words kept echoing gently beneath the surface of my thoughts, reshaping how I saw everything around me.

How could two such different worlds coexist in my life—serving boat-drinks under the warm Hawaiian sun one day, plunging into cosmic mysteries with a telepathic dolphin the next?

Already, I found myself eagerly anticipating our next encounter, curious about what truths she'd reveal next.

As we arrived back at Keauhou Bay, the girls decided to give me the rest of the day off. With no divers on the passenger list, I wasn't needed for the afternoon trip—and they knew I'd been working ten days straight.

What a luxury, I thought, realizing I had the next two days off as well. It had been a while since I'd had that much downtime—and enough money to comfortably pay rent in the same month.

✳✳✳

On the drive home, I stared straight ahead through the split windshield of my '67 Volkswagen camper van, lost in thought. Afternoon sunshine had given way to familiar *mauka* showers—those tropical rains that rolled in like clockwork over the coffee belt's upper slopes. My wipers beat a steady rhythm, a metronome for my conflicting emotions.

I kept grasping for rational reasons to seek Deja out again—as if my decision wasn't already made. Even so, I needed to convince my logical side.

I wanted to know her purpose.

I needed to know—why me?

What could I possibly offer?

But what scared me most—ironically, considering the subject of our last conversation—was the possibility that she might ask me to *do* something. Being with Deja was exhilarating—almost addictively so. But the idea of becoming some kind of dolphin disciple, preaching cosmic truths to the world?

That just wasn't me.

I kept thinking, *I'm a dive guide on a snorkel boat. What could I possibly say to influence human nature after eons of ingrained behavior?*

More than anything, I needed to know who she was.

Strangely, the thought of talking to a dolphin seemed harder to accept than the idea of conversing with some otherworldly intelligence about the universe's grand design. And, for reasons I couldn't quite explain, that unsettled me most of all.

By the time I turned down Napo'opo'o Road, my emotional side had done its job—arming my rational side with just enough justification to go back.

Only this time, I'd be prepared.

This time, I'd get the answers I needed.

✳✳✳

The next morning, I snorkeled out to the usual spot—though I'd slept in and taken my sweet time getting to the beach. I was experimenting. We had no appointment, no set plan. I just had this intuitive sense that she would appear if I sought her out alone. That's how it worked last time, and that's what I was testing.

Sure enough, as I approached the underwater ledge, Deja rose up from the blue. Before she could even flick her tail, I reached for her dorsal fin, my heart racing as she whisked me deeper into our surreal world of discovery and wonder.

This ride was faster—more intense—than before. I streamlined my body, held my mask in place, and cleared my ears rapidly and often. Deja seemed to know my limits—giving me the thrill of speed without exceeding my comfort zone.

I remember thinking—*everyone should have their own playful pet dolphin.* What a way to start the day.

After a short spell of underwater barrel rolls, she surfaced so we both could breathe. Several deep breaths later, we descended again, leveling off at about 30 feet and lazily cruising our way toward the mouth of the bay.

She said nothing at first, but her joy radiated into me—like sunlight through water—lifting my spirit, dissolving every trace of concern.

I sometimes wondered why we didn't talk on the surface. Later, I was glad we didn't. Over time, the dolphin pod in K-Bay became well known, eventually falling under the Marine Mammal Protection Act. Interacting with them became illegal under certain conditions, and my connection with Deja could easily have been misread as harassment. Besides, surface activity attracts boaters, fishermen, and curious beach-goers. Looking back, I see now that she was avoiding scrutiny.

But in that moment, I wasn't thinking about any of that. I was just enjoying the ride—the freedom of long dives, untethered by tanks or by time.

Finally, she broke the silence.

"Patrick, you seem disturbed today."

"Huh?"

She was referring to my earlier mood. But at that moment, I was exhilarated. Who wouldn't be—after a joyride that got my adrenaline pumping like a firehose and my heart grinning like an idiot?

I'd nearly forgotten what I'd been brooding about.

"Oh, yeah... it had something to do with, uh..." I hesitated, trying to phrase my thoughts delicately—pointless, of course, since she already knew exactly what I was thinking. She must have seen me as an exercise in patience, waiting for my mind to catch up.

"Deja, what exactly are you going to ask me to do with this information you're giving me?" Frustrated, I dropped the pretense and just said it.

"Learn it."

"Then what?"

"Live it."

"You don't want me to teach it?"

"It's okay to teach it. Just be careful not to preach it. The last thing you want is to start a religion."

I got the sense she wasn't joking.

"The best way to teach is by example—live it."

"But Deja, that sounds like a really slow process for solving our problems. Wouldn't it be faster if we just told people?"

I caught myself. Here I was, arguing for exactly what I had been trying to avoid.

"When you live something, it is noticed. Your vibrational field affects all matter around you. It cannot be ignored. Love sends a vibration. Fear sends a vibration. Trust sends a vibration. These vibrations accumulate, gaining momentum, becoming a powerful force. They affect all energies at the intra-atomic level."

My mind snagged on the term, *"Intra-atomic?"*

She elaborated.

"These vibrations arise from subtle energies existing between physical particles—in spaces that seem empty, yet hold tremendous power."

I smirked. *"That sounds like a pretty tight fit to me."*

"Actually, this space is immense."

I remembered the last time I asked for an example and braced myself.

"Give me an example."

This time, her delivery was gentler—but just as dramatic.

"Picture an atom the size of a massive domed stadium. The nucleus would be the size of an olive. The electrons, like grains of sand. Everything else? Space. And within that space dwell energetic life forces. They cannot be measured. They are not material—but they exist, and they influence everything around them. These are the subtle energies many of you are just beginning to perceive."

I was still absorbing this when she pivoted back to my earlier complaint.

"The slow process you refer to is an ignorant reference to what you call time."

Before I could bristle at the word ignorant, she flooded me with warmth—dissolving my desire to take offense.

"The human mind has existed on this planet for about a million years. If that entire span were measured on a 24-hour clock, the average human lifespan is less than seven seconds."

Suddenly, I saw it clearly—history whizzing by at hyperspeed, generations flickering past in the blink of an eye.

"Social progress is always hindered by the demand for change within the span of a single lifetime. But society cannot cope with rapid change—even when the change is good."

"But Deja, if we don't change quickly, we're going to ruin the planet."

"Indeed. It's a fine mess you've gotten us into, Stanley."

I blinked. Was she quoting Laurel and Hardy?

It unnerved me how casually she treated the looming crisis. But before I could respond, her tone softened.

"Regardless of urgency, the only way to bring about major change in a single lifetime is through force. And forced change never lasts. It's human nature to resist force. Try forcing a child to eat candy—you might just create an aversion to sweets."

Her point was clear: even the best ideas meet resistance when they're forced—often before their benefits are even considered. I imagined even the wheel would've been rejected if early humans had been forced to adopt it in the span of a single lifetime.

My mind wandered into the absurd. I pictured some heavy-handed "Law of the Wheel" mandating every household own a minimum number of wheels—each bearing a legally specified percentage of the family workload. Citizens forced to attend 'Benefits of the Wheel' propaganda courses. Congregations kneeling at the Altar of the Sacred Spokes. Praising the god of circular salvation.

Naturally, people would hate it. Not because the wheel lacked merit—but because it was imposed, not chosen. Eventually, I saw the revolt—an uprising against the tyranny of the wheel. The masses uniting in the 'War of the Wheel,' rejecting their overlords' masterplan in favor of a liberating alternative.

Perhaps a spring-loaded pogo stick—freedom's triumphant bounce against circular tyranny.

Just as I reached peak absurdity, Deja pulled me back.

"It might serve you to know," she said, *"that what you call 'original sin' had something to do with an attempt to engineer significant change within the span of a single human lifetime."*

Her emotional field dimmed. Not from withdrawal—but from reverence. I felt she was brushing the edge of something sacred…or perhaps still under celestial embargo.

My curiosity surged—but she offered little, as if speaking more would trespass against some ancient covenant.

"Had wisdom and patience prevailed 38,000 years ago," she continued softly, *"your world would be a very different place. But what's done is done."*

A flash of *missed-opportunity* flickered between us—like the echo of something precious, once within reach, now exiled in time.

"The question remains," she said calmly, *"when will humanity learn that lasting change must unfold across generations? Major shifts need time—to take root, grow strong, and become stable if they are to become socially sustainable. Demanding otherwise is folly—selfish, even. And ultimately, counterproductive."*

I let out a breath. She had told me all she was willing to.

"Why are we so obsessed with seeing change in our lifetime?" I finally asked.

Her field opened again—steady, loving, and clear.

"Because your impatience comes from spiritual immaturity."

I felt her pause, as if to make sure I wasn't taking it personally.

"You crave recognition, personal validation. You desire the satisfaction of witnessing change yourself, rather than cultivating change that endures."

"Guilty as charged," I thought, as she continued.

"True progress is always generational. And knowingly pushing for immediate results at the expense of long-term well-being—even with noble intentions—is not merely unwise… it is evil."

Her words landed hard.

In that moment, I saw with startling clarity how even the noblest goals—if pursued through flawed, impatient, or forceful methods—can sabotage the very outcomes they aim to achieve. Rushed change never yields lasting results. It fractures the foundation beneath it.

And suddenly, everything clicked into place.

The end never justifies the means—because misaligned means can distort, diminish, or destroy the very good we hoped to achieve.

Worse still, any attempt to shortcut what Deja radiated as a sacred, divine process… is the very definition of evil.

She gave me space to sit with that truth—to really let it settle deep within.

And I had to admit… it *felt* right.

But I was still troubled by the urgency of the human condition. If our greed is driving extinctions… if our planet is teetering on the brink… if fear itself is killing us—shouldn't we be doing something now?

Deja, always tracking my thoughts, replied, *"That is correct. You should* **start** *doing something about it now. Now would be a very good time to start."*

"Well, what should we do?" I asked.

"Good question," she replied. *"But before I answer, let me ask you something more important: How soon do you expect to see significant progress?"*

"Well, soon, of course… certainly before I die, I would hope."

The words slipped out instinctively—then immediately I realized I'd stepped into her trap.

"I see you're not ready for the answer to your first question yet," Deja chuckled gently. *"It's frustrating to see the sky falling when you don't know what to do about it. But it's useless to know the solution if you lack the patience to let it work."*

I winced. She was right. Even after our talk about time and generational change, my knee-jerk reaction had betrayed me. Old habits really do die hard.

"Okay, so how long should it take?" I pressed.

"That depends on the problem," she replied.

"There seem to be so many… it's hard to know where to start."

"True," she agreed. *"And too often, your solutions focus on treating symptoms instead of addressing the root cause. But let's say you set out to intentionally engineer a society designed around natural law and long-term sustainability—a socially moral society. One that needs few laws and minimal enforcement. A society*

that embraces science and innovation to ease hardship, yet lives simply, spiritually, for the common good... in harmony with the planet."

"Deja, is that even realistic?" I asked, skeptically. *"Utopia sounds amazing, but humans are... well, human. Can't we start smaller? I mean, a moral society? That's a big ask."*

She replied with the tenderness of a teacher, patiently guiding me toward discovery.

"Argue for your limitations, and you'll surely get to keep them.

"Believe in your potential, and your faith will move mountains.

"Are you not astounded by what the human mind has accomplished in just the past few centuries?"

I couldn't argue. I just listened, as the truth of her words settled in.

"Who's to say your society couldn't one day engineer a shared morality—by consensus, and by conscious design?"

Then came the images—rapid, powerful flashes—revealing just how many problems a genuinely moral society could solve. I didn't want to admit it, but she had a point.

"Okay," I sighed. *"Assuming it could be done... how long **should** it take?"*

"Barely seven centuries—if you start today," she replied with serene confidence. *"Easily within the next millennium."*

I was stunned!

Forever! ...that's what I was hearing.

"Uh, Deja... that seems like an awfully long time."

"Only about sixty seconds on our 24-hour clock," she replied joyfully.

Then she added, pointedly, *"Of course, if that feels too long to wait, you're free to continue as you are. You may keep chasing hastily contrived quick-fixes and never reach your potential—not in seven thousand years—or even seventy thousand."*

She wasn't mocking me or even challenging me. She was simply stating the truth—with tenderness and gentle honesty. The choice was ours. We'd be loved either way. But there was no mistaking which path held wisdom.

I tried to wrap my head around seventy thousand years in either direction. It was too much—my imagination buckled. It just couldn't stretch that far.

Then, right on cue, Deja cut in playfully.

"Even that is just a hundred minutes on our 24-hour clock."

Put that way, seven hundred years didn't sound quite so brutal. Still, I couldn't shake the disappointment.

"It's tough to pour your heart into something when you'll never see the results," I thought.

"You forget," she said gently, *"that life—both physical and spiritual—is a journey, not a destination. How do you know you'll never enjoy the benefits? Don't you feel something when you give a gift, even when you receive nothing in return?"*

"Well... yeah. Actually, I do."

"How can that be? You weren't the receiver. You didn't get anything."

I paused. *"I don't know. It's not tangible. But sometimes, I feel like I enjoy giving more than the other person enjoys getting."*

She let me sit with that thought for a moment, then continued, her tone, soft but sure.

"Some lessons in this life directly prepare you for the next. The joy you feel when giving—it's not just a pleasant emotion. It's a clue. It reveals the deeper power of altruism—its superiority over fleeting material satisfaction."

I nodded, soaking it in.

"Each time you give unselfishly," she said, *"you also receive. That's not metaphor. That's universal law. It transcends the temporal. It's subtle proof that spirituality exists."*

She paused again, and her next words rang out like a calling.

*"To take part—**freely**, **humbly**—in something that benefits future generations? That's one of the highest acts of service possible on your planet."*

I felt a stir in my chest—something between humility and awe.

"And that service," she added, *"doesn't disappear. It carries forward. It shapes what comes next. The joy you feel when you give? That's only a glimpse of what awaits as your spirit grows beyond this world."*

She slowed our glide almost to a stop, to let me and the moment breathe—then brought it home.

"So, circling back to your objection—you will enjoy the benefits of your labor. But only if your labor is unselfish... and unselfishness," she added with a knowing warmth, *"requires patience."*

As I absorbed her words, something clicked: there's no shortage of people who desperately want the world to get better **now**—in their lifetime—preferably before the next election. Waiting isn't part of their plan.

"That must be frustrating for our leaders," I reasoned.

"Indeed," Deja agreed. *"Your leaders are in a difficult position. They can accomplish no more than they're allowed to. If the populace is impatient, the leaders cannot be effective. Lasting change takes time—and it cannot come before, or exceed, the education level of the average citizen."*

That hit me harder than I expected.

"If the citizens are ignorant, they become easy prey for simplistic, short-term fixes—the kind usually offered by corrupt and ignorant leaders."

Deja let that truth settle. Her silence was intentional—like a teacher giving the lesson time to land.

Then she continued.

"Regardless of your currently popular political fantasies, a society can only be as good as its average members. At best, your leaders will be only slightly more ethical than the general population—especially in a representative government. The key to better leaders is a socially moral and well-informed public."

"But that's not what people want to hear," I said.

"And for a long time, people refused to hear that the world was round," she quipped. *"It didn't make it any less true."*

"This will take time," I thought.

"That's right," Deja responded cheerfully. *"A short seven centuries ought to do it nicely."*

I couldn't believe she said *"short."*

"I'm sorry, Deja, but that still feels like an awfully long time. I don't think people are willing to wait that long. What about passing laws to speed things up?"

I felt her sigh knowingly, like a patient parent preparing to explain—for the hundredth time—why the child can't have dessert for dinner.

"Deterrent force might change behavior temporarily—but it doesn't transform people," she said gently. *"Those who intend to harm, exploit, or manipulate will always find a way."*

She paused, letting that truth settle.

"Social morality cannot be mandated—it must be chosen. The instant it's forced, resistance follows."

I started to respond, but she continued, reading my thoughts before they took shape.

"Laws can support progress—but they're not a cure-all. When they multiply beyond necessity, they become a burden—draining energy, time, and resources from the very systems they're meant to protect."

At that moment, she projected a vivid image into my mind: a highway system where every driver followed the rules—not out of fear, but through shared understanding.

No speeding tickets. No radar traps. No overburdened traffic courts.

The savings were staggering. Resources once spent on enforcement now went toward better roads, smarter infrastructure, and public education—social solutions. Former enforcers turned their energy toward building instead of policing.

And it all worked because people had chosen to drive responsibly—not because they were forced to, but because they understood that doing so benefited everyone.

Elevated morality led to smarter systems, lighter workloads, and more meaningful leisure time.

"Morality is a freewill matter," Deja continued. *"It's personal."*

I tried to imagine how that kind of shift could spread. *"If not through laws... then how?"*

"It spreads best through example," she answered, *"from highly moral individuals to those still searching for universal truth."*

Even though that made sense in theory, a part of me still whispered that maybe a few well-placed laws might help get things moving—at least in the beginning.

"Laws should only be enacted with overwhelming consensus," she said, *"and gradually phased out as morality takes root. "Above all, the law must never evolve into an industry—a self-serving societal malignancy that spreads through civilization like cancer through a body."*

The image came vividly: a vicious cycle of multiplying laws—each spawning clarifications, amendments, new enforcement agencies, and endless loopholes. A system spiraling out of control, burning itself out just to regulate its own complexity. We weren't just on the path to that trap—we were already in it. We built the maze, and then got lost inside.

Still, I kept circling back to that seven-century timeline, like a bad song stuck in my head, while Deja crystallized the connection between law and morality.

"Within the universal law of cause and effect," she said, *"you'll find the extent of civil regulation is inversely proportional to the morality and ethics of its citizens."*

That truth caught me off guard—but it explained a lot. She was saying that socially immoral societies require a flood of laws, while moral societies barely need any at all. By that standard, we weren't just circling the drain—we were halfway down. Self-policing felt like a joke without a punchline. Seven hundred years? Oof—try never. But—as always—Deja had a way of reframing things.

"You're obviously too young to remember," she teased, *"but it was only 531 years ago that Gutenberg reinvented the printing press."*

"Reinvented?" I blinked. *"I always thought he invented it."*

"Movable type originated in China centuries earlier," she corrected gently. *"But that's beside the point. Just over five centuries ago, most people were illiterate. Only the wealthy could read, and books were rare—painstakingly copied by monks.*

"Now," she continued, *"just 46 seconds later on our 24-hour clock of human history, literacy is the norm. Imagine being dropped into the 15th century—before Gutenberg—and telling scholars that one day, everyone would read."*

I thought about it, then grinned. *"Well, if they didn't know Gutenberg, they'd probably picture a future crawling with monks, scribbling day and night."*

I felt Deja's snicker—several rapid-fire clicks and a high-pitched squeal. Then it hit me. *"Forty-six seconds? When you put it like that—it really wasn't all that long ago."*

"Nor will a minute be," she gleefully added, *"when your world stands at the threshold of your unfolding utopian society."* I noticed she'd said **when**—not *if.*

"Although you may not realize it," Deja said lovingly. *"you're already doing many things right. But you lack patience—like a perfectly designed helicopter missing its tail rotor. Everything else works—it should fly—but without that essential piece, it spirals out of control and crashes. Sometimes catastrophically. Worse, even, than if it were flawed from the start."*

She paused to let the image settle. *"In many ways, your societies are like children who don't understand why they must wait to grow up. And like that helicopter, they crash—again and again—until they finally discover and add the missing pieces."*

Then, with a graceful flick of the tail, Deja slipped my grasp and circled around to face me—head-on—as if to underscore what came next.

"Your perception of time is myopic. It will sharpen after you pass beyond this lifetime. In the context of eternity, solar revolutions are a blur—like the blades of a fan spinning on high. The bigger picture is so much more than a single lifetime's journey around your star. To believe otherwise is like calling the universe 'flat.' If your world is to reach its potential, you must evolve your relationship with time."

And, then in a flash, she returned to the blue as I steadily kicked myself up to the surface—her parting message echoing in my mind.

Chapter 6

Threshold

The next morning, I could hardly wait to meet Deja again. I woke at the first glint of sunlight poking through the cracks in the single-wall construction of my two-story shack. Buzzing with anticipation, I skipped my shower and made a beeline for Glen's kitchen.

He was already up, cooking his eggs and getting ready to play captain on the Fair Wind.

"You workin' today?" I asked, just to make sure he wouldn't be around to see me sneak off with my snorkel gear.

"Yep—for the next three days. Giving Liz some time off," he said, flipping his eggs. "What are you doing today?"

"I dunno," I lied, trying to sound casual. "Day off. Probably just putter around here."

"So why you up so early?" He paused, giving me a look. What I'd said didn't add up.

I shrugged. "Habit," I mumbled, and changed the subject. "Mind if I use the toaster?" I nodded at the finished toast still hogging the slots.

"Sure," he said, grabbing his and moving aside.

"How many you got this morning?" I asked, meaning the passenger count.

"No idea. I'll find out when I get there. Doesn't matter to me, I'm just driving the boat—the crew's gotta do the work." He looked up and smirked as he slid his eggs onto a plate. "Easy duty. Free lunch. Hopefully some babes on board."

I chuckled. As single guys in our late 20s, that was definitely one of the job's best benefits.

"Well, good luck with that," I smiled wryly, cracking my own eggs into the pan.

We made some more small talk, then Glen was off. I scarfed down breakfast, grabbed my snorkel gear, and hustled down the road to the beach, curious—and a little anxious—to see what the day might bring.

✳✳✳

The ocean was flat that morning. Perfect. Entering from the black sand beach was easy, and less than five minutes later, Deja met me—sooner than expected. I hadn't even reached our usual rendezvous spot.

She seemed just as eager as I was.

As we glided silently toward the mouth of the bay, my thoughts kept drifting back to our earlier conversations.

"Deja, the world seems so confused. Some of our problems feel hopeless... is it really possible to work together to solve them? I mean, where do we even start?"

"You have already started."

I blinked. *"Huh?"* That threw me off balance a little.

"I haven't started anything," I said. *"I'm just enjoying a life of fun in the sun."*

"Yes, but what did you trade for your fun-in-the-sun life?"

"A life of chasing dollars?" I guessed. Anyway, that was the way I looked at it.

"Yes, you traded in a life of material aspirations to, let me see... how did you put it when you quit your job? Ah, yes… **'to stop and smell the roses,'** *I believe you said."*

I froze. That was *exactly* what I'd said when I quit my real estate job. Even though I was living a lifestyle that others envied—new home, fancy car, tailored suits, fine dining and money to spare—I felt inexplicably restless.

An inner voice warned me to get out before I got trapped by my own "success." So, I sold everything and moved to an island in the middle of the Pacific.

No plan, no job, no clear vision of what I'd do next. Just a knowing that I needed to escape the hamster wheel… to *'stop and smell the roses'* before I got seduced by the endless, insatiable chase for *more*—the same trap that had already snared so many of my friends and associates.

"How did you know I said that?"

"How do I know anything?"

She had a point. After everything she'd already revealed, this minor detail barely even registered.

The sun was just cresting over the rim of the towering cliff behind us as Deja towed me through the water toward the mouth of the bay. By now, our encounters felt almost routine—though the thrill of riding a dolphin never got old.

It was Tuesday—my second day off in a row—and I was beginning to wonder if I should take a leave of absence to spend more time with Deja. But I needed money for rent, and I wasn't about to risk losing my job on the *Fair Wind*. There were plenty of people who would kill for a position on that boat, and I knew I had one of the sweetest jobs in Kona.

Still, I couldn't shake the sense of uncertainty—of teetering on a threshold between a safe, familiar world and a journey into something extraordinary, yet frighteningly unknown. It felt like a movie that keeps ending with *To be continued…*but I needed to know *what comes next.*

And then there's my fascination with Deja. I had never met any-one—human or otherwise—who could so completely captivate my mind. Her insights lit something up inside me, something I ached to share. But every time I imagined opening up to someone else, a knot twisted in my gut—part fear, part longing. The urge to speak collided with the dread of sounding crazy, or worse, losing the friendships I cared about most.

Picking up on my silent turmoil, Deja continued.

"At this very moment, millions of people across your planet wrestle with the same restlessness as you did. Their intuition tells them there's more to life than material success… and they're searching for it."

"Exactly **what** *are they searching for?"*

She already knew what I was about to ask, of course. But as always, she waited for me to consciously shape the question before answering. I appreciated that—remembering how overwhelmed I was in our first encounter, when she flooded my mind with pure thought transfer.

"Your utopian society, of course. Knowing your purpose, your origin… your true identity. Happiness. That **is** *what you want, isn't it?"*

"Well, yes… of course. But isn't that what people have always wanted?"

"Indeed. Yet an increasing number of people now realize true happiness won't be found in material things. They're looking inward, beyond possessions, for deeper nourishment."

I could feel the truth of her words resonate through me as she continued.

"You're entering a fascinating new age—one that's well-documented throughout the universe, but still unfolding here. An age where scientific discovery and social advancement will merge with your search for spiritual identity—launching your per-spective to the next plateau of social vitality."

Whenever Deja hinted at life beyond our planet, I usually tried to humor her. It was hard to take the cosmic stuff seriously. But this time, something shifted. I couldn't shrug it off—my mind demanded clarity.

"Deja… are you saying the path we're on has been walked by others before?"

"Not the exact path," she said. *"But the epoch you are entering is familiar ground. It is well understood by those who've observed or experienced it."*

"Wait... so we're not alone in the universe?"

"Of course you are not alone. Don't be silly." I could feel her chuckle rippling through me."

"How could you possibly think all this creation is just for you? All those galaxies, stars, planets—sprinkled across the sky— just a fabulous backdrop for late-night stargazing?"

She was shamelessly mocking me—and I couldn't help but smile.

"Well, I've always had a feeling there might be life out there, but—"

"Not only are you not alone," she cut in, her voice laced with amusement, *"you're not even particularly advanced. The physical world you perceive is just a speck—like a dust particle under a microscope, clinging to an entire planet you can't see... because you simply can't zoom out far enough."*

She was still snickering.

"If these beings are so advanced, why don't they make themselves known? Why don't they help us create a better world?"

"You are being guided far more than you realize. But there is much you must discover for yourselves. Haven't you noticed that when you tell someone how to do something, they rarely learn it as deeply as when they figure it out on their own?"

"Well... yes, I have noticed that."

"And when you struggle to understand something—really work at it—you tend to value that knowledge more, don't you?"

"Yes. In fact, when I've earned it, I'll even argue for it."

"How astute."

She was actually complimenting me. I felt a small surge of pride as she continued.

"That's because you've tested it. You know it's true—not because someone told you, but because **experience** *made it yours."*

I nodded, as she added, *"A wise teacher guides you to the edge of discovery. Simply handing out answers robs you of the deeper understanding that only comes from the journey. The struggle clarifies the problem. And when the solution finally arrives, it's not just an answer—it's a transformation."*

As she paused, I felt it—the transformation gradually unfolding within me as she patiently guided me along my own path of discovery.

"And then, once learned, that solution sticks. It becomes repeatable, adaptable. One doesn't just gain an answer—they gain a **process** *they can use again and again."*

It made perfect sense. She was showing me that real understanding must be **earned**—not given.

If higher intelligences simply gave us answers, we'd stop learning our own lessons. We'd grow dependent—a kind of cosmic welfare state. I could already see how quickly we'd start expecting that kind of help.

I imagined the abuses in my head. If we needed a new energy source, why bother with research? Just ask the aliens how to harness the sun. Conserve? ... Nah—just give us more power.

We'd become like those who wanted Christ to perform miracles, but showed no interest in his teachings. I smirked inwardly, thinking, *"Yeah, never mind the hard part—just bring on the miracles. Hand us the keys to the cosmic candy store—fix our problems. Quickly... today would be good."*

I amused myself, but Deja let it pass without comment.

It was clear how fast we'd become addicted to having our problems "fixed." Even now, most people assume science will eventually solve everything—but few understand how, or even care to learn. They're just waiting for the next miracle. Deja was right. We're not ready. No intelligent ET in its right mind would reveal themself to us publicly.

"Deja, tell me about the other planets… what are the beings like on the advanced worlds?"

In a tender whisper, she replied...

"Patrick, if you listen carefully, you will find I **am** *telling you."*

"Oh."

I was little embarrassed I hadn't realized that.

"The Creator designed a universe where humans with spirit-potential learn by insight as well as experience. That's what separates you from animals—who learn

only from experience. Humans can look before they leap—and learn from both the looking and the leaping.

"Animals must leap before they learn. And those of higher intelligence, through experience, may even achieve a goal by selecting a means.

"But humanity can examine the goal itself, evaluate the means to achieve it, and even question whether the goal is worthy in light of the methods required to reach it."

I started to wonder where she was going with all this. I was engaged—but I was also beginning to feel… lost.

We'd covered human restlessness, other planets, utopian societies, higher consciousness... and yet, I thought we were talking about fear. Honestly, it was becoming a lot to process.

She must have sensed it, because just then, Deja began to thread it all together.

"The universe isn't a finished painting—it's a living canvas, always reaching toward perfection. It wasn't designed to be flawless, but to grow. Had your world been born without evil, ugliness, or hate, you'd never know the transcendent power of truth, beauty, and goodness—realities that rise, take root, and blossom into love."

She paused, then shifted gently from the universal to the personal.

"If your world is to evolve—to truly move forward—you must not only understand the root of your problems, but also the purpose behind them. Just as physical symptoms fade when the body heals from its underlying illness, so too will countless human dilemmas vanish when you finally learn to subdue your fear."

I felt her words land—quiet and true—settling into some deep, receptive place inside me.

But still, I remained stuck on the most basic question.

"So… how?" I finally asked, the voice in my head barely more than a whisper. *"How do we subdue our fear?"*

"By altering your perspective of death."

"How do we do that?" I pressed.

"By transforming your relationship with it," she said gently. *"By seeing this life as preparation for something greater—a journey beyond this existence."*

My chest tightened. *"But Deja… that's going to take a massive leap of faith."*

I could feel her inner smile, her warmth washing through me like sunlight filtering through the shallow sea.

"Exactly," she said, with a note of satisfaction.

"And that brings us full circle."

We drifted in silence, our movement nearly still—carried by a grace only a dolphin could know.

And slowly, it all began to click.

This was why she had redefined time… why she'd emphasized patience, linked mortality with spirituality, and hinted that we are all being guided toward something greater.

Piece by piece, her words wove together like threads of light, forming a pattern so vivid, I could almost reach out and touch it.

It all pointed toward one thing.

Faith.

The spiritual equivalent of splitting the atom, inventing the wheel, harnessing electricity, and taming fire.

I remembered asking, *"Where do we start?"* and Deja responding, *"You have already started."*

I saw that now. The better question was, *"Where do we go from here?"*

"Ahh… yes, an inspired question."

I could feel her joy as she spoke the next sentence slowly.

"I have been hoping you would ask."

She spoke like a Zen master recognizing a student's readiness for the next level. After a long pause, her tone grew more solemn than I had ever felt before.

"What I am about to share with you, many are not yet ready to hear."

I gave her the attention of someone about to be entrusted with a secret.

"Your present circumstances on this planet are urgent yet opportune. Since comparatively few of you are yet receptive to these truths, you must remember that— **it will do more harm than good to force these truths upon others.**

"First, you must share these perspectives gently, clearly—and then step back. Allow others the freedom to choose their own path.

"Success will require a heightened degree of patience and a broader perspective of time.

"Do you understand?"

My throat tightened, as if I'd swallowed a stone. I felt a pulse quicken behind my eyes. She was going to ask me to share all of this publicly—I just knew it. The thought of stepping into that spotlight, of risking ridicule, losing my friends, even jeopardizing my job and identity terrified me beyond reason.

I could almost hear the mocking laughter of Glen and the skeptical silence of Deb, feel the friendships I cherished fracturing into awkward distance.

It struck me just how rich the irony was. I'd once abandoned everything comfortable, to seek a simpler truth—and here I was again, facing another leap. Only this time, the stakes felt cosmic.

Yet, I knew if I resisted, our encounters might end. And by now, I craved her revelations more deeply than I cared to admit.

She waited.

"Yes... I understand." I was trying hard not to seem tentative.

Deja resumed speaking in her familiar feeling tones—love, peppered with excitement and enthusiasm.

"You... all humanity stand on the threshold of a new era; an era of great learning. A renaissance of philosophy, morality, brotherhood, and spirituality. An era through which you must pass in order to reach your final destiny as material beings—to become settled in **Light.***"*

She heard my mind ask, *Light?* The word echoed like a tuning fork. A strange, euphoric sensation washed over me, as if the word itself held a charge, vibrating with some truth my body remembered but my mind had yet to grasp.

"To explain such an era would not do justice to this final epoch of advanced evolutionary planets. Yet, I can say, you would certainly call it 'heaven on earth.' It is known to the universe as the culminating era of human evolution."

I listened intently as Deja continued.

"At some point in your future there will come an Assembly of Great Teach-ers... and the time to prepare for their coming has never been better. You have many circumstances in your favor... more than you might imagine.

"For the first time, you can communicate efficiently across the globe. Science is advancing rapidly, and your inventions have removed much of the drudgery from life. Some of you are discovering the value of productive leisure—essential for moral, philosophical, and spiritual growth. You also recognize the importance of educating the average person, though this remains one of your greatest challenges.

"Peaceful cultural exchanges are taking place, and ideas are being shared more freely. Economic trade is beginning to outweigh nationalistic ego. Your races are slowly assimilating, language barriers are thinning, and representative government is evolving—despite its flaws and the refinements still to come.

"These are advantages your world has never known on a global scale—tools you can use to overcome your greatest challenges. Within your grasp lies the potential for global peace, ethical society, a high quality of life for all, and the leisure to pursue philosophical and spiritual truth.

"Yet just as surely, great hurdles remain—ones you must acknowledge... and overcome."

"Such as?" I was fascinated and excited.

Then she enthusiastically rattled off the downside.

"In general, your morality and ethics remain deeply flawed. You are spiritually confused and fragmented. Your religions are rigid and divisive. Your planet is over-populated, and you are depleting its resources at an unsustainable rate. Your science has yet to seriously address your inherited biological limitations. Many of your so-cieties continue to subjugate women. You speak multiple languages, and your con-flicting social philosophies and cultures cause constant misunderstandings."

"Geez, anything else you want to throw in?" I groaned sarcastically, se-cretly hoping she'd laugh or at least lighten the mood. Right on cue, I felt her gentle amusement ripple through me as she continued lovingly, her tone honest yet almost apologetic.

*"Yes. Your diversity, though beautiful, has made unity more difficult. However, your solutions must be guided by empathy, compassion, and love—intelligent assimilation—**certainly not by force.**"*

She spoke cheerfully, radiating reassurance.

"Throughout the universe, no world has ever reached its settled era of Light without first establishing a common language, a shared morality, and a unified philosophy."

I felt my stomach tighten. *"Deja, you're asking too much. People aren't going to agree on one language, one morality, or one philosophy—and certainly not one assimilated culture!"*

I couldn't believe it... she seemed genuinely delighted—like a child who'd led a friend to hidden treasure.

"How can you be so positive in the face of such major obstacles?"

Tenderly, she answered, *"Patrick... it's not impossible. With every problem comes opportunity and discovery. And honestly? I find that exciting. Don't you?"*

Exasperation rose from within. Exciting? Was she serious? I felt like I'd just been handed a bomb with instructions to look for the hidden gift.

"Opportunities, yes. Discoveries... maybe. Problems? No... I don't. In fact, I don't like problems at all. And I especially don't like emotionally charged problems... and, uh, Deja... I think you struck the motherlode of emotional landmines!

"Congratulations. If anyone is listening in, we could be killed within the hour."

I could tell she was ignoring my drama.

"Every problem bears the gift of knowledge. And, assuming you wish to acquire the lifestyle of a morally, philosophically, and altruistically advanced society, these are facts you must know... and obstacles you must overcome. The Assembly of Great Teachers will not arrive until the average person is aware of these truths and ready to make progress toward a socially moral and ethical society."

"There's got to be another way," I tried to think privately.

"Certainly. You may continue indefinitely your current method of adjusting misunderstandings born of national pride and cultural fears through the arbitrary outcomes of physical combat."

"War?" I thought.

"However," she continued, *"it's doubtful The Great Teachers will arrive anytime soon since war is so unimpressive—having been discredited long ago as a method for settling differences on civilized worlds."*

She was genuinely sincere, and I couldn't resist her optimism flowing into me. Even so, I could never see myself coming forth with these revelations. They seemed so unsettling to people's current beliefs. I wouldn't begin to know where to start. My mind conjured up images of being outcast if I even mentioned her disclosures in a public forum.

"Patrick, remember—time and patience are your allies. Faith is a tremendous lever. Just as the seeds of literacy were planted in the 15th century only to fully blossom in the 20th, the seeds of Light are being planted now. Nurture these seeds lovingly with faith, courage, wisdom, and patience, and they will blossom in the not-so-distant future, eventually bearing a lasting fruit that will fully ripen in the following millennia."

I swallowed. *"Is this something that you know will happen... or is it just a theory?"*

"It is a fact that settlement in Light is your destiny. You are, in fact, standing at the threshold of a great learning epoch... yet there is no guarantee you will pass through the door at this time. I can tell you there is much work for you to do and great curiosity throughout the universe as to which way you'll choose. If you follow your inner-guides, you will persevere. If you succumb to your fear, you will find yourself rebuilding again... and again, and again—perhaps not always from the beginning, but certainly from a point of significant regression."

Once again, she broke from my grip and circled around to face me.

"We have arrived at a time when you, dear Patrick, must make a personal decision. I am willing to assist you with reconciling the challenges of these obstacles, which are significant, and provide you with insights for overcoming them. However, you will have to decide for yourself if you want to know these answers."

"Are you inviting me to drink from the fountain of knowledge?" I was trying to lighten the tone, but we both knew we were serious.

Unfazed, she replied with a tenderness that made the ocean itself seem still.

"Yes... and with it will come the responsibility of knowing... and, eventually, you will be compelled to share that knowledge. Or, on the other hand... we can end our encounters and say it's been fun... as we both know it has been."

After about a minute of silence, I heard her say...

"I will know your answer if we meet again."

With that, she disappeared into the blue, leaving me alone as I kicked my way toward the surface, breathless—not just from lack of air, but from the weight of realization that the next breath I took might carry me across a threshold... into a life that could never return to what it was before.

Chapter 7

Leap of Faith

I kept replaying everything Deja had said. My recall was uncanny—not just the words, but the cadence, the feelings, the layers beneath. Each scene unfolded in my mind as if I were reliving it in real time. It felt otherworldly. Unsettling. Yet it was also the very thing that kept me from dismissing our encounters as a dream.

More and more, I wrestled with the possibility that Deja wasn't just a dolphin. Maybe she was an illusion. Or an intelligence from somewhere else… appearing as a dolphin.

Either way, I was captivated.

She understood our world—deeply. And she was willing to share that knowledge with me.

I didn't care what she was. Illusion or not—appearing as a dolphin? Brilliant. Who could resist a telepathic dolphin? Certainly not me.

Still, some of what she said… the world wasn't ready for.

I could accept her critiques on ethics and morality. No problem there. And I agreed that our religions are rigid and intolerant.

But when she spoke about *biological limitations*, the *barrier of multiple languages*, or *intelligently assimilating conflicting cultures?* These are the things people go to war over.

And yet—even when I bristled—her voice would echo back in my mind:

*"Your solutions must be guided by empathy, compassion, and love—intelligent assimilation—**certainly not by force.**"*

That word—*intelligent*—kept pulsing. She didn't mean intellect. It was something *measured, deliberate, tested.* A weaving-together forged through patience, and agreed upon by those qualified to decide.

I felt it in her tone. The compassion. The tenderness. The *urgency.* And always, that echoing refrain: **Barely seven centuries ... only sixty seconds.**

She wasn't calling for a revolution. She was calling for deliberate, consensual change—born of education, not coercion.

And in that context... it seemed *possible.*

Not a fantasy. Not a dream. Something that could actually take root.

Even though I wanted to push her words away... I couldn't. I knew they were true. They just felt... *right.*

Still... being the one to bring her message to the world?

To stand there, exposed, a target for every skeptic, every cynic, every self-appointed executioner of impossible dreams?

Hell. No.

That would be suicide.

The struggle churned in me like a riptide—weeks of avoiding the bay, burying myself in work, stacking shifts, dodging the water.

I even lied about an ear infection so Deb would take my dives— and noticed her and Liz exchanging worried glances behind my back.

I imagined the skeptical stares, the whispers—friends who wouldn't—or couldn't—understand.

The ocean, once my sanctuary, now loomed like a cathedral of secrets—holding truths I wasn't sure I wanted to uncover.

It wasn't Deja I feared. It was the weight of *knowing more.*

Finally, after nearly a month, fear lost its grip, yielding to clarity—and a gnawing curiosity about what lay ahead.

I decided. Tomorrow, I would return to Deja. Ready or not. And this time... I wouldn't just listen. I would cross the threshold. I would drink from the fountain.

Chapter 8

The Other Side

As Deja rushed toward me from the depths, I reached out, catching hold of her dorsal fin as she glided past. To my delight, she spun me into a series of barrel rolls, the water rushing past us like a river and sweeping away my dive mask.

Then she picked up speed. Faster. Then faster still. I felt the pressure shift as we broke the surface, expecting the familiar slap of reentry into the sea. But instead—

A burst of white light!

A powerful force surged beneath me, lifting me skyward. Deja's pectoral fins stretched outward, morphing into vast, feathered wings—impossibly white, smooth as polished marble, spanning over thirty feet. Her sleek gray form shimmered, then dissolved into a cascade of silken feathers. Her neck, strong yet graceful, arched with the elegance of a stallion in motion.

I instinctively wrapped my legs—fins and all—around her midsection, grabbing a handful of her soft, feathery mane for support. My breath quickened, my heart pounding, and my hands trembled as I tightened my grip. My stomach flipped—not from the height, but from the surreal shift in reality. For an instant, panic gripped me before awe swept it gently aside.

For the first few minutes, I couldn't speak, my thoughts swirling wildly. I closed my eyes, took a steadying breath, and cautiously opened them again.

The ocean was gone, replaced by rolling emerald hills, crisscrossed with winding streams and glistening lakes. The air tasted fresh, almost sweet, filled with unfamiliar floral notes that made each breath seem cleansing.

The land stretched endlessly below, lush and teeming with life—trees, plants, birds, and animals I couldn't name. Everything was unfamiliar yet felt so benign... and spectacularly beautiful.

As I reached down carefully to ditch my fins, a question surfaced in my mind.

"Who are you?"

"I am who you think I am." The tender voice was Deja's.

I recalled one of my first ever questions to her and repeated it. "*What* are you?" This time it seemed more appropriate.

"I am a fandor, of course," she answered.

I shook my head slowly, disbelief battling with awe. Finally, almost whispering, I managed to voice the obvious question:

"Deja... where have you taken me?"

Her gentle voice, now audible and impossibly calm, drifted through the air.

"We have arrived on the settled world of Avona."

It was the same familiar voice, soft and feminine, but for the first time I was hearing it with my ears—and the realization sent a thrill through me.

I opened my mouth, then closed it again, words failing me. My heart thumped loudly, not in fear, but in astonishment and wonder. I took another deep breath, letting the fragrant air and incredible reality sink in.

"Avona," I murmured, testing the strange name on my tongue. "Another... world?"

"Yes," Deja said simply.

I laughed softly—part disbelief, part exhilaration. Yesterday, my biggest worry was tourists kicking coral reefs. Today I'm *flying* on a... "What did you call yourself?"

"A fandor," she said softly, amused.

"Right, a fandor." I chuckled nervously. "Next you'll tell me mermaids are real."

Deja's laugh, light and melodious, rippled through me. "Let's leave some surprises for later."

Grinning widely, I replied "Fair enough—but if unicorns show up, I'm officially calling this a dream."

My heart rate was finally starting to normalize. The enormity of the moment began to settle within me, not all at once—but slowly, gently, making space for whatever this amazing world had in store.

As we soared, I marveled at the passing landscape, the wind whipping gently through my hair. Below, in a meadow, a herd of zebra striped animals resembling miniature giraffes grazed on the tall grass like shrubs.

They had long necks and legs, yet their bodies were ostrich-like. They were covered with neither fur nor feathers, yet I couldn't call it skin or scales either. What came to mind were leaves... very thin, broad leaves that, by jostling in the breeze, exposed a multicolored underside, producing a rippling effect.

It made the animals seem animated even when they stood perfectly still. Their voices were a lyrical blend of kitten-like mews and birdsong, blending naturally into the harmonious hum of this living, breathing paradise.

Finally, my curiosity overrode my amazement. "Where are we going?" I asked.

"To the city of Pardysia to meet Landorf and Vanatta. You did want to learn about the beings of other worlds, didn't you? I hope you haven't changed your mind about..."

"Oh no... I'm excited, this is great! Please... whatever you have in mind, let's do it."

I knew she was teasing, but I wanted her to know how much I appreciated the ride. Strangely, I never questioned how it happened. Somehow, it felt... inevitable.

The skies were abundant with exotic birds of many colors, sizes, and sounds. It reminded me of the multi-colored fishes on the tropical reefs back home. But K-Bay felt a million miles away, and some part of me had already surrendered to the wonder. Yet, for a fleeting moment, I was half-worried about making it back in time for work on Friday. How could I ever explain this to Deb—she'd probably assume I'd found some seriously magic mushrooms.

Occasionally, we encountered other passenger birds. Deja greeted them in a language I couldn't understand. As they responded, their passengers would smile and wave. Of course I waved back, grinning from ear to ear, delighted to be riding a fandor high above a botanical world so splendidly beautiful.

Time lost meaning as we soared, circled, and glided on the thermals—Deja barely flapping, riding the currents with the same effortless mastery she had once displayed in the sea.

And then, in the distance—I saw it.

A city.

No, not a city—something beyond anything I had ever seen.

The buildings shimmered as though they were spun from jewels—crystals, embellished with precious metals and gemstones. Some were translucent, others opaque, radiating a dazzling spectrum of colors—ruby reds, emerald greens, electric blues, luminous golds—all interwoven into an enormous architectural mosaic.

Parks, gardens, amphitheaters, open-air plazas—all arranged with such remarkable precision it felt as if the city had been conceived in a single moment of divine inspiration. Nothing out of place. No signs of decay or neglect.

But it was the people that caught my attention most.

Even from above, I could see there was something different about them. Their movements were fluid, purposeful—unhurried yet efficient. Unlike the bustling crowds back home, there was no chaos, no frantic energy, no sense of strain. They appeared to go about their activities with an ease that felt... intentional, as if every step was part of some unspoken rhythm the entire society understood.

Having surveyed a portion of this great city's edge, we spiraled high over the center. Below I saw what appeared to be a gigantic, circular glass lake, flat like a mirror—yet I knew it wasn't water. I guessed it to be about 10 miles in diameter, and gasped when I laid eyes on the brilliant gold amphitheater that surrounded it. It was **immense**. I thought to myself, *this structure could seat a million people!*

After reveling in the most breathtaking of views, we glided down and landed delicately at the very center of this mysterious glass object.

"Welcome to Avona's capital city of Pardysia."

Deja stooped down and I slid off her back, my bare feet contacting the impossibly smooth surface. I could feel a subtle energy vibrating beneath me. The sensation was unlike anything I had ever experienced—an almost electric hum that permeated deep within.

"Deja, what is this, uh... thing we've landed on?"

She turned to me, her expression serene. "This is called *The Crystal Sea*—an enormous, polished crystal used for many purposes. Dignitaries arriving from other worlds are welcomed here."

Her words took a moment to register. "Dignitaries from other worlds?" I repeated in disbelief.

"Planetary gatherings of universal importance also take place here... and it functions as a vast resonator—like a cosmic tuning fork—broadcasting and receiving messages across the local universe."

"Universal broadcasts?" I let out a breath. "Whoa! ...that's *incredible!*"

"Why have you brought me here... to this planet?"

"Experience is always the best teacher. You will soon see why you are here."

I glanced around, fighting the urge to question how any of this could possibly be real. Yet somehow, everything around me defied disbelief, settling comfortably into a space within me that felt right. Even hearing Deja's voice—now emerging from the elegant, winged creature she had become—felt as familiar as breathing.

Then, something even stranger happened. As I stood barefoot on the smooth crystalline surface, I felt... different. Lighter. Clearer. Stronger. When I looked at the back of my hand, I saw scars from recent coral scrapes fading away until they were gone—and there was no trace of the slice on my finger that I got while chopping pineapple on the boat a few days ago. It seemed like I was being *repaired*.

It wasn't just my body that felt whole—something in me, old and broken, had quietly mended.

"Deja," I said, staring at my hands in astonishment. "This crystal... what is it? I feel like I'm healing all over."

She answered only by saying, "Are you ready to meet Landorf?"

"What's a Landorf?" I smile teasingly.

"*Who's* Landorf," she corrected, grinning slightly.

"Oh.... well then, *who* is Landorf?"

"You will see." She smiled back.

Unlike Deja the dolphin whose face was fixed in a perpetual smile, Deja the fandor showed expression. Her features—somewhere between avian and feline—reflected warmth, intelligence, and an unmistakable playfulness. When speaking she smiled naturally while her eyes twinkled affectionately.

"Climb aboard," she said, her voice a gentle melody that resonated with the surrounding tranquility.

Deja crouched slightly, allowing me to ease myself onto her back and get a firm grip on her soft, feathery mane. Two steps and a powerful leap, her enormous wings unfolded, and we were airborne once again, soaring into the boundless sky like the Pegasus of legend. I couldn't help but wonder if those mythical flying horses were actually passenger birds, gone extinct long ago in the midst of some ancient human conflict.

I waited, half-expecting Deja to comment—but she remained silent. Only the wind replied, as if some mysteries were meant to linger.

The landscape below unfolded like a living masterpiece. From high on the outskirts of the great city, I could see a village emerging in the distance. Translucent dwellings without roofs, nestled amid the rolling hills—each structure harmonized with the lush greenery and colorful gardens surrounding them. Unlike Earth's chaotic urban sprawl, everything here flowed. As if the architects had studied nature, and decided to cooperate instead of compete.

Streams and ponds wove throughout the scenery, their surfaces mirroring the sky's hues, shimmering with every subtle breeze. The bridges looked organic—rooted into the banks like living extensions of the terrain. Vibrantly colored walkways meandered purposely, their colors shifting subtly as if they were alive. There was no friction—only form, balance, and breath, as if the entire setting exhaled in harmony.

We soon circled a courtyard at the heart of the village, descending toward two figures who stood waiting below. They looked up with warm smiles, their hands raised in greeting as if they had been expecting us. As we landed with effortless grace, I slid off Deja's back, my feet touching the soft ground just as the gentleman stepped forward. With a gesture as familiar as it was reassuring, he extended his hand— offering me a firm, welcoming handshake.

"Hello, Patrick. My name is Landorf. This is my wife, Vanatta. Welcome to our home."

I shook his hand—warmth radiating from his touch. His eyes— calm, wise, utterly sincere—stirred something in me, an inexplicable trust, like I'd known him forever.

"Thank you, Landorf. Nice to meet you, Vanatta. I feel so privileged to be here."

A fresh wave of exhilaration surged through me—I'm actually on another world… meeting the locals.

Vanatta, radiant and statuesque, greeted me with a warm hug and handed me the robe she'd been carrying. Only then did I realize how out of place I must've looked—barefoot, in swim trunks, standing on an alien world. I slipped into the elegant garment with a grateful nod. I wasn't cold, but something about dressing like my hosts made me feel more grounded—less like an alien myself. As I adjusted the sleeves, I couldn't help but wonder if they saw me the same way I sometimes saw tourists on the *Fair Wind*.

I declined the sandals she offered, preferring to remain barefoot and savor the feel of the plush courtyard beneath my feet. It was cool and soft like close-cropped grass—the kind you would find on a putting green—yet its intricate design reminded me of an exquisite Persian rug.

As I squatted to examine the texture and design, Landorf turned to Deja and greeted her in a foreign tongue. She responded graciously in English.

"Thank you, Landorf. It is good to see you both again. If you don't mind, I have matters to attend to while the three of you become acquainted. Call for me when I am needed, won't you?"

Landorf and Vanatta smiled and said they would. With that, she took off again—this time with speed and power, a stark contrast to the gentle precision she'd used to lift me skyward.

As I turned back to Landorf and Vanatta, I studied them more closely. They were undeniably human, yet there was something... beyond. Their skin, a seamless fusion of earthly complexions, carried an iridescent sheen—subtle hints of violet and gold catching the light.

Landorf stood tall and broad-shouldered, his crystal-blue eyes a striking contrast to Vanatta's deep, earthy green. Both were taller than anyone I'd known, their medium-length, golden-brown hair framing features untouched by age or wear. They radiated an effortless vitality— an almost ethereal presence as if time and illness were foreign to them.

I had no idea what was coming next, but I knew one thing for certain—I had crossed a threshold into something extraordinary.

As the three of us strolled toward a round table beneath a gazebo, I found myself marveling at the climate. The air was neither too warm nor too cool, carrying the faintest hint of floral sweetness. From the surrounding trees came the lilting calls of exotic birds—soft trills, cascading whistles, and playful notes that danced through the air like living wind chimes. The gardens stretched in perfect harmony, their colors rich and vibrant, untouched by decay. Even the atmosphere seemed... serene, as if the very concept of disruption had been erased from existence.

Vanatta watched my fascination with an amused smile. "The weather here is constant—it never deviates. We don't experience storms, rain, or snow like you do on Earth, and there are no seasons as you know them."

"Ahh, so that's why all the buildings are roofless?"

She gave a knowing smile and nodded.

And then the thought occurred to me, "So, how do you water your gardens?"

"Our water cycles naturally through streams, canals, and subterranean aquifers. At night, precipitation forms when an additional inert gas in our atmosphere raises the dew point."

I turned the thought over in my mind. No forecasts, no hurricanes to brace for, no blistering summers or brutal winters. At first, it sounded like paradise. But then another thought crept in—don't they ever miss change? Would endless perfection start to feel... stagnant?

Landorf, sensing the shift in my thoughts, smoothly redirected the conversation. "Deja tells us you're troubled by the social obstacles your world faces."

Vanatta studied me with quiet curiosity. "Is this true, Patrick?"

Still riding the mental sharpness I'd felt since stepping onto *The Crystal Sea*, I answered without hesitation.

"Yes, actually I am. I'm particularly disturbed by her claim that one of our greatest obstacles to achieving a moral and ethical society is our failure to address our biological limitations."

They listened intently, their expressions open, waiting. No judgment, no shock—just patience.

"Even if she's right," I continued, "I don't see how we could ever convince my people to address something like that. It's too... charged. I mean, on my world we can't even get a group to agree on pizza toppings."

They both smiled politely, but if they found it amusing, they didn't show it.

"Anyway, it seems pretty clear to me that imposing it would only lead to disaster."

Landorf nodded. "You're correct. It cannot be forced without causing social upheaval."

He paused before continuing with a casual patience, "But all life inherently seeks to improve itself. Nature is designed for progress. The evolutionary drive toward perfection exists across all worlds."

I wanted to argue, but something about the way he said it made me pause. He spoke with such certainty, yet his delivery carried the same compassionate warmth and loving intonations I had grown so accustomed to in my interactions with Deja.

"Evolution," he went on, "typically occurs through natural selection—survival of the fittest. In the animal world, if a species cannot adapt, it ceases to exist. But humans—on any world—are unique. We are given the ability to intervene in this process by making intelligent choices."

I tilted my head slightly. "Intelligent choices?"

Vanatta took over seamlessly. "Unlike animals, humans can make choices that affect their biological future. You have already begun this process."

I blinked. "We have?"

Vanatta nodded. "Of course. The moment humans began intervening in life's natural processes, you embarked on the path of intelligent choices."

As I absorbed her words, the surroundings momentarily faded, only to return sharper than before—colors vivid, scents richer—as if understanding somehow heightened my senses.

Landorf continued, "That does not mean your choices have always been wise. Far from it. But the fact remains—your species has already begun shaping the trajectory of your biological future."

"Patrick," Vanatta's voice was smooth, deliberate yet full of warmth, "You do this every day—through medicine, through technology, through the increasing control you exert over birth, life, and death."

She spoke slowly, letting each sentence settle like dew on a still morning.

"Even the foods you manufacture and the diets you cultivate shape the biological future of your species. A role that once belonged entirely to nature now rests, in part, in human hands."

I frowned, trying to digest the meaning of their words. "So, you're saying we're already engineering humans?"

Vanatta nodded. "Yes, and with profound consequences—both physical and societal. Whether intentional or not, every intervention you make in birth, health, and survival shapes the trajectory of your species."

She studied my expression, sensing my hesitation, and continued gently.

"When you sustain life that nature would have otherwise taken, you alter the course of evolution. When you extend reproductive privileges to those unable to contribute meaningfully to society, you shift the genetic landscape. Every decision—fertility treatments, medical advancements, dietary choices, even how you distribute resources—plays a role in shaping the biological and ethical future of your civilization."

I exhaled, her words settling in with me as I finished her thought out loud, "…while, animals are at the mercy of natural selection …they can't actually control their evolution, can they?"

"That's right," Vanatta gently affirmed. "But humans can. We have the ability to make deliberate choices—yet on your world, you wield this power without coordination, without foresight. You react to problems instead of planning for sustainable progress."

She paused, watching me, perhaps noticing my unease. Then, with quiet patience, she leaned in slightly, her voice softer yet steady. "You possess extraordinary tools, but you use them haphazardly—without a guiding principle to ensure they truly serve the greater good."

I understood her words, even agreed in theory, but the idea of implementing such change on my fractured, strife-torn world felt impossible—like trying to steer a storm with bare hands.

Landorf's gaze was steady, his voice genuinely curious. "What puzzles us most is why a species as intelligent as yours has yet to recognize this responsibility. You hold the power to uplift future generations—not through force, but through foresight and wisdom. And yet, you resist even the discussion."

I thought about the starving populations we struggle to sustain—our compassion undeniable, our intentions noble—yet the cycle of poverty continues. I cringed at the vast resources poured into prolonging life for the terminally ill, even as education, innovation, and infrastructure—the very tools to shape a better future—remain underfunded.

"We do it in the name of compassion," I offered. But even as I said it, a thought lingered: perhaps it's as much about easing our own conscience as it is about helping others.

Vanatta's gaze remained warm, but her voice carried a quiet weight. "And yet, in time, your descendants may say, *'Your compassion lacked wisdom.'*"

She allowed a moment for the thought to take hold before continuing.

"True compassion does not simply ease suffering in the moment—it seeks to prevent it in the future. But too often, your world makes decisions based on short-term emotions rather than long-term vision."

I was clearly being taught, yet it never felt like a lesson. My hosts carried a rare blend of patience and insight, sensing my thoughts and emotions with uncanny precision. They weren't just speaking *to* me—they were guiding me, tailoring their words to match my understanding and my capacity to consider new ideas.

Sensing I was ready for more, Landorf continued, his voice calm but firm.

"Every human, on any world, influences the collective destiny of their civilization. It is an inescapable truth of interconnectedness. Society is not defined by its exceptions but by its majority. And when that majority is guided by ignorance, moral decay, or spiritual apathy, collapse is inevitable. This is not philosophy, Patrick. It is natural law—cause and effect as predictable as gravity."

As had always been the case with Deja, Landorf and Vanatta tempered their words with deep compassion. There was no judgment, no superiority—only patience and a sincere desire to guide me through the labyrinth of my own doubts. Their words resonated beyond logic, carried by something deeper—an unshakable sense of truth.

After a brief but meaningful silence, Vanatta spoke again.

"To shape the course of human evolution is not an act of tyranny, but a natural prerogative of intelligent life. It is the very thing that separates the spiritual mind from the animal brain. But power without wisdom is reckless. The ability to intervene does not grant the right to impose—it demands responsibility. True progress is not about forcing change but fostering it—wisely, patiently, for the sake of future generations."

They always picked up effortlessly where the other left off, their thoughts seamlessly interwoven. No competition, no urgency to speak first. Perfect synchronicity. Calling their relationship 'beautiful' felt inadequate. It was something more. It was… *exquisite.*

Continuing Vanatta's thought, Landorf explained, "There are constants in the universe—unbreakable cause-and-effect relationships. Some are obvious. When someone jumps, gravity ensures they return to the ground. No law needs to enforce it; no decree can override it.

"Even if a government mandated that people must not land after jumping, nature would pay no heed. Natural law always prevails over civil law."

I scoffed. "Yeah, but that's ridiculous. No one would ever pass such a law. ...I mean, gravity is self-evident. It's everywhere."

Vanatta nodded. "Of course. No one doubts gravity—it proves itself every time we fall. But not all truths are so obliging. Biological, sociological, and spiritual laws are just as real, but harder to observe—and so they're often ignored or misunderstood on your world."

"Just like the laws of electricity before they were discovered," Landorf added. "For centuries, humanity had no concept of the forces that now power your entire civilization."

He leaned forward slightly. "The same is true for these other universal laws. They exist with the same certainty as gravity or electricity—yet take time to observe, and longer still to fully comprehend. A cause will always lead to its effect, yet without a long-term perspective, societies often fail to recognize the patterns at play."

I smirked. "So, you're saying we have a short attention span?"

They both smiled at my attempt to lighten the mood but chose not to answer, letting the weight of the conversation linger.

A few moments passed before Vanatta added, "Deja has asked us to share with you some of these natural laws."

I exhaled, already suspecting where this was headed. "Let me guess—our biological messiness is at odds with natural law?"

Their knowing smiles confirmed what I already understood. No need for words—they knew I had grasped the connection.

I sat quietly for a moment, watching a flock of small orange birds land a few feet away in the courtyard. They looked like finches—at least, close enough—and for a moment, I felt a strange sense of comfort. Something familiar in a world where *almost nothing* was. This minor familiarity anchored me before I spoke.

"Alright... even if I accept, in theory, this is true, I just don't see a way to guide my world toward addressing these biological concerns."

Vanatta's expression remained warm but firm. "Patrick, what you've just said is like saying, 'Even if I accept that gravity exists...' Natural law does not require belief to function. It simply is. Whether acknowledged or ignored, it remains constant."

I could feel myself tense a little. "Where I come from people hold passionately to beliefs rooted in compassion, even when those beliefs might inadvertently sustain the very problems they long to solve."

I think my frustration was beginning to show when Vanatta added a gentle reminder.

"Their compassion is commendable, but it often lacks wisdom."

I wanted to push back—but couldn't. Deep down, I knew she was right. Compassion alone wasn't enough. Without wisdom, it could become dangerous.

Vanatta waited patiently for me to process my thinking before continuing.

"Two plus two will always equal four. No amount of belief or opinion will change that. A society that votes to make it five may succeed in shaping perception, but their miscalculation will eventually collapse the system built upon it. Do you understand?"

I nodded slowly. They weren't trying to convince me of anything—they had no need to. They were simply guiding me toward conclusions that, on some level, I already sensed. There was patience in their teaching, a willingness to let me arrive at understanding in my own time.

"I think I get it," I admitted. "You're saying that reality doesn't bend to human perception. That natural law is immutable. And when we act in ways that contradict it, we inevitably face the consequences."

"Exactly," Vanatta affirmed tenderly, her voice calm but resolute. "A civilization cannot thrive if its course is misaligned. Just as a spacecraft requires a precise trajectory to reach its destination, so too must a society follow a carefully charted biological and ethical course if it hopes to evolve toward stability and enlightenment."

She let her words take hold, giving me a moment to absorb the weight of the idea. Then Landorf added another layer of perspective, offering a simpler analogy.

"As bricks are to a building, individuals are to a civilization. A structure built on weak bricks will crumble. Your world now possesses the knowledge and technology to reinforce its foundation—if it chooses to begin by studying the process."

I leaned back, thinking out loud. "Now that's something I can live with... *studying the process* **first**, without rushing into action. We don't have to do anything drastic."

Landorf nodded approvingly. "That is the only way forward. Any attempt to impose change quickly or by force will fail."

Vanatta added, "And right now, your planet suffers a severe shortage of those truly qualified to make such determinations. Your greatest challenge is not merely implementing change, but cultivating the wisdom to guide it."

Landorf's tone remained calm but pointed. "However, in time, as understanding deepens, your world may come to accept the idea that certain hereditary conditions and profoundly antisocial traits should not be perpetuated—not through coercion, but through a collective recognition of what fosters a stronger future."

I had no objection to eliminating inherited diseases—if we had the means to prevent suffering, why wouldn't we? But the idea of addressing antisocial traits in the same way had never crossed my mind. Could such tendencies really be passed down, just like physical traits, or was it more complicated?

Landorf, responding directly to my thoughts, explained, "Temperament is largely inherited. Those prone to antisocial behavior often pass those tendencies down, just as those who are socially well-adjusted instill in their descendants an inherited inclination toward cooperation and responsibility."

It was something I'd noticed—how children often mirrored their parents' emotional patterns. I'd always assumed it was learned behavior. But Landorf was suggesting it could also be inherited.

Vanatta leaned in, her expression intent. "The distinction is simple: those who value life seek to nurture it—to build, to contribute. Those who do not—who prey upon others without conscience—become a destabilizing force. They shatter trust, magnify fear, and consume far more than they return."

I was beginning to see where this was going.

Landorf continued, "Conversely, those who cherish life and the well-being of others, form the foundation on which civilization can flourish."

As before, they gave me a few moments to absorb their words. When I tilted my head and nodded, they took it as a sign to continue.

"In the absence of those who disregard life," Vanatta added, "societies find their natural rhythm. War diminishes, security concerns fade, and the need for excessive laws begins to disappear. A culture that respects life is one that thrives."

I sat there, trying to grasp what they were teaching me. They weren't speaking of control or purging—not in the tragic ways history has misused such ideas—but of recognizing long-term patterns, about preventing predictable cycles of harm.

The idea seemed simple in theory: if humanity removed its most destabilizing influences—not through force, but by consciously shaping its future—I could see how that could accelerate its evolution. And yet, the complexity of such a shift felt staggering. Could we ever make such choices wisely?

Even amid the wonder of Avona, one thought haunted me: if this knowledge was truly meant for me... was I strong enough to carry it?

How could I ever explain this back home without sounding insane—or worse, dangerously radical?

A soft hiss pulled me from my thoughts. I turned to see a fine mist shimmering over the mosaic walkway, catching the light like dusted glass. Another whisper of water followed, washing down the gazebo's pillars in a thin, shimmering sheet. Yet, strangely, the water never pooled. Instead, it disappeared into the surface like magic, leaving no trace of dampness behind.

I frowned, glancing down. The walkway was dry—almost as if drinking in the moisture the moment it touched. My expression must have given me away because Landorf shifted effortlessly into an explanation.

"You see, most things here are alive on some level... including much of what we build."

I knelt, running my hand along the mosaic path. It looked like a colorful mix of polished quartz, but the texture was something else entirely—firm yet yielding, like springy rubber. Curious, I reached for one of the jade-like pillars. To my astonishment, it was pliable, with faint white veins threading through its surface, pulsing ever so slightly. My mouth fell open. I turned in a slow circle, suddenly hyper-aware of my surroundings, half-expecting the very walls to be watching me in return.

Landorf chuckled. "Yes... almost everything."

I turned back to him, still reeling. "What about the translucent buildings?"

"The crystallineum? Oh yes, that too—organically engineered crystal." He gestured around us, his voice warm with quiet pride. "We don't just construct—we cultivate. Each creation is a collaboration with nature, designed to flourish in perfect harmony with the world around it."

That explains why nothing here shows any sign of wear—no cracks, no weathering, I thought idly.

"That's right," Landorf confirmed, reminding me once again that my thoughts were not private. "And because we understand the composition and needs of each life form, we can shape them to fit our environment. Size, structure, texture—all tailored without compromising the integrity of the living material."

He gestured toward the path beneath my feet. "By the way, this walkway is edible. Though I do have better food to offer."

Still grinning at the idea of edible walkways, I watched Landorf retrieve a small basket from a nearby alcove. Inside was what appeared to be fruit. My curiosity, however, was briefly diverted when I returned to my stool... or rather, what I thought was a stool.

Now that I was paying attention, the flat-topped green cushion looked distinctly like a giant mushroom. I bent down, examining the soft yet structured ribs underneath. When I lifted it, I found it to be surprisingly light.

"They're called stootles," Landorf offered casually. "We use them because they thrive in low light, they're easy to move, and... well, they don't seem to mind being sat on. Plus, they naturally conform to our shape."

I hesitated for a moment before lowering myself onto the strange, living cushion. The surface adjusted beneath me, subtly shifting to accommodate my weight. A small shiver ran up my spine as I registered what was happening—this thing was alive. It wasn't unpleasant, just... strange. I exhaled, shaking my head in amazement before finally reaching for the fruit basket.

"Stootles, huh? Bit of a missed opportunity—you could've called them 'fungi-ture,'" I muttered, mostly to myself.

Vanatta let out a soft, surprised laugh while Landorf chuckled, eyes twinkling, "I'll consider recommending that to our council."

Their amusement lingered as they watched me pick out what looked like an apple, hesitating only briefly before taking a bite. Immediately, my wariness faded. It was sweet, crisp, and bursting with flavor. Easily the best apple I had ever tasted.

Landorf's smile widened. "Some things can hardly be improved."

I laughed quietly, grabbing something that resembled a plum. Again, it tasted as it should—like a plum—but sweeter than any plum I could remember. Only after I had devoured both did I realize something odd.

"They're seedless," I murmured, more to myself than anyone else.

Landorf smiled knowingly but didn't answer. Instead, he stood and gestured toward a winding pathway that disappeared into a vibrant tapestry of blossoms and foliage beyond. "Patrick, would you like to go for a walk in the garden?"

"Oh, yes... certainly. I would actually... I'd like that very much."

Vanatta graciously excused herself. "I hope you don't mind, but I have some things to attend to inside. If it's all right with you, I'll listen in from a distance as the two of you continue talking."

I thanked her for her insights as I wondered how, exactly, she would follow our conversation without being present. Regardless, I trusted that she could and decided not to question it.

Curiosity tugged at me, stronger now, as I followed Landorf toward whatever revelations awaited—aware, perhaps for the first time, that I was stepping into a truth that, once embraced, would forever shape my future.

Chapter 9

The Garden Path

The gravity of our conversation still clung to me, but something about the garden's quiet harmony made it easier to think—easier to breathe.

The path meandered through a botanical wonderland, teeming with vibrant, otherworldly flora. The colors—spectacular. The fragrances—intoxicating. The names—mostly unpronounceable, at least for me. Landorf, however, rattled them off effortlessly, as if he had named them himself. Only a handful bore any resemblance to the flora of Earth.

He spoke with the pride of an artist unveiling his life's work. But these weren't just plants to him—they were living compositions, each element cultivated not in isolation, but in conscious harmony with the others. The way he described their intricate relationships—their mutual support and interdependence—made it clear this wasn't mere horticulture. It was a living tapestry of color and form, meticulously arranged, masterfully balanced.

Yet, even as I admired the garden's perfection, my mind remained tangled in the complexities of our earlier discussion. I could grasp the logic—how a civilization could advance once it embraced the sanctity of life. But how does a world get there? *Natural law. Inherited temperament.*

The idea that *compassion without wisdom* could be dangerous. It all made sense in theory, but in practice? It felt impossible.

I exhaled, rolling these thoughts over in my mind before finally voicing my frustration.

"Landorf, even if I agree you're right, I just don't see how we'd ever be able to get from where we are to where we need to be."

Landorf walked beside me, hands loosely clasped behind his back, his gaze moving over the garden with quiet reverence. When he spoke, his voice carried the kind of patience that made me feel he would wait however long it took for me to grasp his meaning.

"Patrick, the first step is education," he gently advised. "A society that understands these truths will, over time, reshape itself. Through its own choices, it will foster stability and ethical progress. Within a few generations, you will see the corrosive forces of corruption, deceit, greed, and exploitation begin to wither—not by force, but by the natural consequence of shifting values. When humanity becomes aware of the long-term impact of its decisions, it begins to act with greater wisdom."

He paused, reaching out to touch a delicate bloom, his fingers grazing the petals with noticeable admiration. The moment stretched, offering me space to absorb his words before he continued.

"What you may not yet realize," he revealed, "is that a civilization built on a stronger biological and ethical foundation will naturally seek higher meaning. A society that is physically and morally sound does not stagnate—it aspires. It is drawn toward greater understanding, toward spiritual discovery. This is not coincidence; it is an inevitable progression. Unless your world makes this connection, true and lasting progress will remain out of reach."

I frowned, looking down while tracing a line in the mosaic path with my toe. "And what if people never recognize it? What if we just keep repeating our mistakes?"

Landorf didn't hesitate. "Then, like every great civilization before yours, it will collapse under its own burden."

A sense of foreboding crept over me. "Do you know that for certain, or is it just your opinion?"

His gaze didn't waver, but his tone was gentle—like a parent explaining a hard truth to a child coming of age. "It's not an opinion, Patrick. It's a pattern—one written into history time and again. When more than half a population operates in fear, greed, or apathy, the balance is tipped. And when that happens, civilization crumbles. It's natural law." His voice held a quiet certainty, almost apologetic, yet unwavering.

A chill crept up my spine as my mind sifted through the wreckage of Earth's past. Rome, Persia, Greece—all once mighty, now just ruins on a tourist map. Each one thought they were different. Each one believed their time would never end. Could we really be next?

I exhaled, raking a hand through my hair. "Alright, I get it. But you have to see the position this puts me in."

For the first time since arriving on Avona, I felt a flicker of fear.

"The world I come from isn't open to discussions like this. Any suggestion of guiding human reproduction—of limiting who can and cannot have children—is seen as a violation of fundamental human rights. Even bringing it up invites accusations of tyranny, of playing God. It's been used to justify horrors in our past. People would see this as no different."

Landorf studied me with quiet understanding. "Your concerns are not without merit. The wounds of your history run deep, and your people still operate from a place of fear—fear of death, fear of oppression, fear of change.

"They conflate equality of the soul with equality of the body. They equate patience with stagnation and resistance with virtue. And because they do not yet understand time as we do, they demand immediate results—sacrificing wisdom for urgency."

He waited for the words to take hold before continuing. "This is why Deja has shown you a broader perspective of time—why she has revealed the truth of existence beyond death, the importance of long-term vision, and the necessity of measured progress. The average person on your world must come to understand these things before they can begin to grasp the responsibility of shaping future generations with intention rather than impulse."

A quiet overwhelm stirred within me. Everything Landorf said made sense—achingly so—but it clashed with a raw truth I couldn't ignore: *my world felt galaxies away from even beginning to move in the direction he was describing.*

The gap between vision and reality felt like a chasm too wide to cross. Landorf, sensing the churn inside me, gave me space—an unspoken grace—to let my emotions rise and settle into the truth. Only when I was still again, did he speak.

"You may be interested to know," Landorf said gently, "that your world is now closer to redemption than it has been in 38,000 years."

A flicker of recognition stirred. Deja had said something similar. My brow furrowed. "What happened 38,000 years ago?"

But like Deja, Landorf let the question drift past—unacknowledged, yet not unanswered. The weight in his silence confirmed what I already sensed: this was a wound not easily reopened. Whatever happened back then, it still echoed.

That silence between us lengthened, but it wasn't empty. It carried significance. Reflection. The steady rhythm of our footsteps filled the space as we followed the curving path beneath a towering arch of flowering vines. Blooms the size of my outstretched hand cascaded in waves of color, their fragrance deepening in the warmth of the late afternoon. A soft breeze stirred the foliage, sending ripples through the lush canopy overhead, as if the entire garden were breathing in unison.

I turned to him. "What about human rights?"

Landorf met my gaze, his expression unreadable, waiting. He knew exactly what I meant but was giving me space to fully form the question myself.

I sighed. "On my world, human rights are an endless battlefield. Hardly a day goes by without heated arguments. Many—perhaps most—would reject the changes you suggest, seeing them as violations of individual freedom."

Landorf's response was measured. "Do your descendants not deserve to be born with sound mind and body? Into a world of moral order and opportunity?"

"Well, that sounds good in theory," I admitted, "but if it means restricting someone's right to have children—or worse, deciding who lives or dies—my people would never accept that."

Landorf's tone remained calm. "Doesn't that seem shortsighted?"

"Um… well, sure. Based on what I've learned from Deja… and from you? Yeah, I guess it does. But really… it doesn't matter if I agree. I just don't see how my world could ever be convinced to embrace such a radical shift"

Landorf nodded thoughtfully. "Patrick, remember—time and patience are your greatest allies. Sudden, forced change is the enemy of true progress."

He walked a few paces ahead before turning slightly, his voice taking on a firmer edge.

"There are two kinds of human rights: individual rights and species rights—self-preservation and species preservation. But often, they conflict. There are times when individual desires must yield to the health of the whole—just as a single infected limb can imperil the whole body, unchecked individualism can threaten the vitality of a civilization."

I had to concede. That made too much sense to not be true.

"What any society calls a 'right' is often just a mirror of its prevailing attitudes. Nature, in its neutrality, grants no automatic privileges— only life itself, and a world in which to live it. Beyond that, civilization must choose—guided by conscience—when and how to extend protections or responsibilities to those whose conditions might otherwise limit their contribution or endanger collective well-being.

"In such cases, only the moral compass of a society can justify overriding nature—and only when done with compassion, wisdom, and care for the greater good."

He glanced at me, studying my reaction before continuing.

"Consider your planet's European Middle Ages, when men were owned as property and had only the privileges granted to them by rulers or religious leaders. That error in thinking eventually sparked rebellion in the opposite direction—toward the equally erroneous belief that all men are created equal.

"That pendulum has now swung fully in both directions. But one day, it will settle in the middle, where the truth lies: a moral society provides every citizen an equal opportunity to realize their full potential—whatever that may be."

Landorf held my gaze for a moment before adding, his tone measured, "Because people are born with different capacities and potentials, the idea of identical outcomes—or identical rights in all circumstances—is an illusion. A society that demands sameness over fairness risks undermining both justice and progress."

He slowed his pace, gesturing subtly to the flourishing landscape around us. "Instead, a just society should administer the varying rights of individuals with equity and fairness. Society's duty lies in providing all people with the opportunity to sustain themselves, to contribute, and to experience fulfillment. That is the foundation of true human happiness."

The words lingered between us.

The ideas ran counter to everything I'd once accepted—everything my world held sacred. And yet, deep in my gut, I couldn't dismiss them. There was no malice in Landorf's words, no arrogance—just quiet certainty, as if he were merely describing the laws of gravity or the movement of the stars.

And then there was Avona itself. A world so obviously in harmony, so undeniably functional. If these people were wrong—if their philosophy was as misguided as my instincts screamed it should be—then how had they achieved all this?

Landorf, always attuned to my thoughts, spoke as if anticipating my hesitation. "Think of society like a symphony," he pronounced. "Every instrument has its role. If the musicians play whatever notes they please, there's no music—only discord. Rights, like musical notes, must be harmonized, not randomly asserted."

The metaphor landed harder than I expected. I'd always been taught that music was freedom, improvisation. But suddenly, I saw the beauty of restraint—how harmony requires discipline.

Several moments of reflection passed before Landorf summarized our discussion with an exclamation point.

"On Avona, our morality isn't measured by how loudly we assert rights, but by how wisely we fulfill responsibilities. Harmony isn't sameness—it's purposeful difference, united in service to something greater."

I exhaled slowly, dragging a hand through my hair. The way he explained it, it all seemed so evident. Yet all I could think of was the obvious question.

"So… how? How did Avona get… to this?" I swept my outstretched arms across the landscape of the garden.

Landorf nodded, as if expecting my question. "Avona is the product of ages of progress—both social and biological—far exceeding the history of Earth. Like you, we are human, and this world was once much like yours in its early stages. But even here, we are not perfect."

"While conditions like mental illness, hereditary disorders, and debilitating disease have been all but eliminated, we're not without compassion. There are still countless ways to serve and contribute—although we no longer face the extremes of suffering seen on your planet."

I listened, my mind struggling to reconcile what I had always believed with what I was hearing.

Landorf's voice remained steady, carrying no hint of superiority—only measured truth.

"Having long since addressed the causes of generational suffering—genetic, psychological, and social—we find little need for civil laws, and war is merely a fact of history. Yet despite our deep commitment to one another, we remain a highly diverse society of responsibly free individuals.

"For true liberty to exist, freedom must be restrained by responsibility. Unbridled freedom cannot exist."

I frowned slightly. "Unbridled freedom?"

"Irresponsible power, when exercised at the expense of others, becomes unbridled freedom."

"For example, the 'freedom' to kill denies another the freedom to live. A society that permits such 'freedom' invites chaos, for no one is free from the fear of being harmed. Only when freedom safeguards all, can peace become permanent.

"Power, when wielded carelessly, masquerades as freedom. The power to exploit, the power to impose one's will over others—these things are the opposite of liberty. True freedom cannot exist where people are subjected to domination, suffering, or fear.

"Genuine autonomy must be in harmony with responsibility—never at the expense of another's liberty."

He paused, stooping to inhale the scent of a brilliant violet bloom before continuing with patient composure.

"This is not a philosophy, Patrick. It's natural law. The same law that governs the balance of ecosystems, the orbits of planets, the forces that sustain life itself. A civilization that aligns itself with natural law flourishes. One that defies it inevitably collapses."

His words carried a quiet conviction, as if he had seen firsthand what happened when civilizations ignored these principles.

Watching him—this marvelous being who has undeniably lived in a world free of war and suffering—I found myself grappling with something even deeper than his ideas.

What if he's right?

If Earth is to survive—if my world is to reach even a fraction of Avona's peace and stability—then how much of what we've clung to so desperately as "rights" and "freedoms" is actually leading us to destruction?

For a while, we walked in contemplative silence, the heft of our discussion settling between us. The garden around us pulsed with life— the soft rustle of leaves, the distant hum of unseen creatures. Every turn in the path revealed something new—a towering arch of flowering vines, the iridescent shimmer of petals catching the golden glow of the late afternoon sun.

Eventually, Landorf spoke. His tone was casual, but his words were deliberate. "Patrick, tell me… wasn't there a time when people believed the Earth was the center of the universe?"

I recognized the shift in direction but answered anyway. "Yes… during the Renaissance, the Catholic Church, under the Pope, declared it a heresy to claim the Earth revolved around the Sun."

Landorf's gaze sharpened. "And those who spoke the truth?"

"Well, they were labeled heretics. Galileo, one of our greatest astronomers, was excommunicated from the church for saying the Earth orbits the Sun."

Landorf's eyes held mine. "And how long did it take for this religious law to align with natural law?"

"Um…" I hesitated. "I suppose it happened gradually," I frowned slightly, trying to recall. "I don't know the exact timeline, but I do know it took a long time for people to accept it."

Landorf studied me for a moment before asking, "How long has it been since Galileo's excommunication?"

I thought about it. "Roughly 300, maybe 400 years."

"And tell me, Patrick," Landorf asked, his voice calm but pointed, "is it now a law that people must believe the Earth revolves around the Sun?"

I gave a short laugh. "No, of course not. That would be ridiculous. We don't need a law to enforce something that's so obviously true."

Landorf's expression was knowing. "Any more than you need a law that demands belief in gravity."

The realization settled over me, and I let out a breath. "Okay... I see your point—but, it's a little bit... unsettling."

The distinction crystallized in my mind. Natural law exists whether we acknowledge it or not. It does not require belief. It does not bend to opinion.

Civil law, on the other hand, is entirely dependent on collective agreement. When enough people accept a truth that contradicts a civil law, that law becomes irrelevant. But the reverse is never true. No vote, no decree, no cultural consensus can override the fundamental principles of nature.

That was the difference. Natural law is absolute. Civil law is temporary. And maybe that was why so many of our laws felt... arbitrary. They weren't anchored in anything enduring, just the shifting sands of human consensus.

Landorf, attuned to my thoughts, allowed me the space to process. When he spoke again, his tone was patient but firm.

"Human understanding does not create truth—it merely uncovers it. The laws of the universe remain in motion whether you accept them or not. And actions, no matter the intention, always yield consequences."

We continued winding down the garden path, sunlight filtering through a canopy of towering blooms. The air was thick with the heady fragrance of blossoms, each breath filling my senses. A soft breeze whispered through the foliage, rustling the leaves in an almost melodic rhythm. The beauty was undeniable, yet my mind remained anchored in the depths of our discussion. The quiet splendor seemed to sharpen my focus, making the significance of our conversation seem more tangible, more profound—and more undeniable.

Landorf eventually broke the silence, his voice steady yet deliberate. "When humanity aligns its systems with natural law, the quality of life improves. When it does not, suffering compounds. Over time, belief gives way to knowledge, and knowledge gives way to wisdom. But such change does not happen overnight. Just as it took generations for your people to accept Galileo's discovery, so too will it take time for society to recognize other universal truths."

I exhaled slowly, feeling the heaviness of his words settle in my gut—not because they were hard to grasp, but because they weren't. That was the problem. How could I accept something I felt my world was destined to reject?

Landorf gave me a measured look. "Forgive me, Patrick, for being sly. Vanatta and I are students of your planet's history. We know that Galileo's case is not unique. He was condemned for telling the truth—forced to spend the last eight years of his life under house arrest. It took less than a century for his ideas to gain widespread acceptance, yet 342 years before the Church officially pardoned him and acknowledged what had always been true."

I let out a short breath, thinking, *342 years to be vindicated? Perfect. My descendants will thank me from their flying cars.*

Landorf caught the thought and offered a small, knowing smile before pressing forward, ensuring I didn't miss the larger point.

"Your world today resists uncomfortable truths in the same way. People don't hold on to beliefs because they are logical, but because they are familiar. Change threatens the comfort of the familiar, exposing the illusion of security. And so, they fear it. But truth needs no permission. Once it reaches a critical mass of acceptance, it becomes undeniable.

His smile turned wry. "Even so, 342 years is not so long ...barely 30 seconds on Deja's comparative clock of human history. A blink of an eye on the universal scale of time."

I let out a dry laugh. "Great—eight years of house arrest? A three and a half century wait for a pardon? Not exactly what I'd call a bargain."

I had meant it as a joke, but the reality behind my words unsettled me.

Landorf had made it clear— change is inevitable. But at what cost? History is full of those who've challenged deeply entrenched beliefs and paid dearly for it. And I had no interest in becoming one of them.

Sensing my unease, Landorf's gaze softened.

I looked away, unable to meet his eyes even though I knew he could see right through me. Then, in that same quiet way Deja had once spoken to me, he whispered, *"Patrick, your fear is killing you."*

I swallowed, my breath catching slightly. He had said it so simply, yet the truth of it settled deep within me.

"Landorf, you don't understand. On my planet, people have killed over these ideas. And fear of death? That's something I have yet to master."

His expression softened. "Ahhh, yes... death." His gaze drifted past me, as if seeing something beyond my perception. "The liberation of personality from physical constraints. The portal to the next adventure on our Paradise journey. That veiled metamorphosis of spirit into an eternal being."

Then his eyes met mine, filled with quiet curiosity. "Why on Earth do you fear it so?"

I exhaled a short, breathy laugh. "Well, when you put it that way, it may seem a bit silly." I hesitated before adding, "I guess... it's the process of dying that seems so frightening. The suffering. The uncertainty."

Landorf, ever the teacher, offered a different perspective. "Isn't it true that many on your world fear jumping into the ocean?"

I frowned, caught off guard by the comparison—until I saw his point.

It was true. As a dive instructor, I'd seen it countless times. For those who had never experienced the ocean beyond the shore, the idea of plunging into the unknown was terrifying. It wasn't that they couldn't swim. It was fear—plain and simple.

But that same fear kept them from experiencing a magical world teeming with color and life—weightless, fluid, breathtakingly beautiful. I had always thought their fear seemed ridiculous, even irrational. And now, I realized my fear of death must seem just as absurd to Landorf.

"But Landorf… there's still the uncertainty of life after death. I've talked to plenty of people who've jumped into the ocean and returned to tell their story. But I have yet to meet anyone who's ever survived death."

Landorf's smile was knowing. "Yes, indeed. You've met only a fraction of the souls you'll come to know."

A chill ran through me. He wasn't speaking metaphorically. He meant it quite literally—that I had yet to meet those I would come to know in the afterlife.

I swallowed. "I've always thought going to heaven had something to do with living a virtuous life… frankly, I'm not sure I qualify."

There was no judgment in Landorf's expression, only certainty.

"Your Paradise journey is the process of *seeking* perfection. The idea that you'll die as an imperfect mortal and awake as a perfect spiritual being is only a pleasant myth. Unless you reject survival outright, your perfection-seeking adventure continues far beyond this lifetime."

His eyes held mine. "You are *spirit* having a human experience. The only requirement for survival beyond mortal death is faith—your cover charge into the realm of eternal progress. *Faith* is the entire price of admission."

Leaning in slightly, his voice carried the substance of truth.

"If only you could see it, Patrick. If only you could perceive the journey—the adventure—you would understand. The lessons along the way are what make life worthwhile.

"To cower in fear," he added, "is to deny yourself the very journey *you were meant to take.*"

Something in his words took root within me. I felt my pulse slow, my thoughts stretch toward something I couldn't yet fully grasp.

For the first time ever, I wasn't just hearing new ideas—I was beginning to see life differently.

An Evening Under Avonian Stars

We had been walking for what must have been a couple of hours, the conversation winding as intricately as the paths through this botanical wonderland.

Sensing my mind was overflowing with new ideas, Landorf gently redirected my attention to the splendor of the garden. He spoke with the reverence of a composer describing a symphony. To him, these weren't just plants; they were living notes in a grand composition—each placed with care, harmonizing effortlessly with the others. As he described their intricate relationships, how they thrived together and supported one another, it became clear: this was far more than cultivation. It was orchestration.

Then it struck me. The garden's harmony was more than intentional—it was a metaphor for their civilization.

Every tree, every vine, every petal played a role in Avona's delicate equilibrium. Like their society, the garden was a living system of interdependence. Nothing was random. Nothing was wasted. Nature here wasn't conquered. It was understood. It was guided. The foliage, like the people of Avona, thrived in perfect sync.

We paused as the Avonian sun dipped toward the horizon, casting long golden rays across the landscape. The sky ignited in hues of deep orange, rose, and violet. It was the kind of sunset that demanded silence—a moment to simply exist within the beauty.

Then, as night settled in, something else caught my attention.

Three massive stars gleamed in the twilight sky—so luminous I might've mistaken them for moons. Their light bathed the garden in a soft, ethereal glow, illuminating every leaf and petal as if the world itself had been woven from stardust.

Landorf followed my gaze. "Our nights are brighter than what you're used to," he acknowledged. "And that brightness, we believe, shaped us. It calmed our fear of the dark. Made us less reactive. Maybe even more reflective."

I looked back up at the sky—at the vast, glowing canvas above me.

Earth's history had been shaped by fear. By survival. By the desperate struggle to outlast the darkness. But here, on Avona, light was always present—a quiet reassurance that softened their most primal fears. Fascinated by the night sky, I stood in quiet awe, feeling its brilliance washing over me. Everything here was extraordinary. Even the air carried an unspoken serenity—a peace so profound it felt tangible.

And in that moment, I realized with sudden clarity... *I did not want to leave.* To depart might be the hardest thing I'd ever have to do.

Landorf's voice was gentle. "Patrick, it's getting late. I suspect you'd like to rest. Please—stay with us tonight. We can continue our conversation in the morning."

The offer landed like a lifeline. I nearly laughed with relief. "Oh, yes... please. That's, uh... great. And generous of you. Thanks."

Even as the words formed, I realized he had already perceived my longing. He knew I didn't want to leave. He knew I wanted to stay. Still, a small part of me worried I was being presumptuous—practically inviting myself in. If he thought so, he didn't show it.

Within the hour, I was stretched out on an Avonian bed, gazing up at the stars through the open roof of the crystallineum home of my newfound friends—on the outskirts of Pardysia.

A zillion miles from K-Bay. Eons away from the backwater planet I'd always called home.

Chapter 10

A Settled World

The question had been circling in my mind since arrival, and it seemed like the right time to ask.

"Landorf, when Deja brought me here, she referred to the *settled* world of Avona. What did she mean by settled?"

Somehow, I sensed he was waiting for me to ask that question.

"Avona is settled in Light and Life," he replied.

I repeated the phrase silently. *Light and Life.* I had no idea what it meant—but somehow, it stirred something ancient within me.

"The Era of Light and Life is the final phase of planetary evolution," Landorf continued, "when a world has achieved universal peace, stability, and deep spiritual realization."

We had taken a new path through the garden, following a trail we hadn't traveled before. Landorf had something to show me, though he hadn't yet said what. We had just finished breakfast—fruits with flavors that awakened my senses, a warm, spiced grain that left me feeling fully alive, and a drink that seemed to spark every cell in my body. Light, yet deeply satisfying.

I tilted my head, still trying to wrap my mind around his words as he continued. "It's an era when all human institutions, relationships, and systems align with natural and divine law."

I gave a slight nod, opened my mouth to respond, then closed it. I didn't know what to say.

Sensing my struggle, he grounded me in something more familiar.

"Everything we've been discussing—the challenges your world faces now—were once ours as well. We began as primitive humans, just as you did. We stumbled, we fought, we learned. Step by step, through biological, social, and spiritual evolution, we advanced. Every hardship, every test, every moment of growth brought us closer to this reality."

Our route through the garden had been intentional. At the end of the path, the foliage parted, revealing a breathtaking vantage point overlooking Pardysia. The city unfolded before me, its crystallineum structures catching the morning sun. Shifting hues of violet, sapphire, and gold sparkled and danced as the precious gemstones and rare metal adornments reflected the light. The entire skyline shimmered—an architectural masterpiece that felt not merely designed, but gently grown, organically attuned to the landscape itself.

Landorf gestured broadly to this magnificent city, his outstretched hands sweeping through the scented morning air. The flourishing beauty of the garden behind us, the brilliant city before us, the palpable sense of harmony—his point required no further proof.

I was at a loss for words. No exclamation, no cliché could capture this moment. Finally, staring out at Pardysia, I managed just one word:

"**How**?" I whispered, gesturing helplessly.

"Well for starters, our governments are not like yours," Landorf explained. "They are highly efficient, operating solely on the principles of truth, beauty, and goodness. There is no corruption, no political division, no struggle for power—only service."

Always showing patience and never in a hurry to proceed, he paused to ensure I was absorbing what he was saying. My mind flashed briefly to images of endless political gridlock, relentless pursuit of wealth, and power struggles that poisoned Earth's societies. Could we ever leave all that behind?

I knew he was following my thoughts as he continued.

"Leadership here uplifts; it does not rule. A true leader does not seek power, but serves as a steward, ensuring that wisdom, cooperation, and progress remain the guiding forces of civilization."

I exhaled, dragging a hand through my hair. "And what about wealth? Power? Don't people still compete for resources?"

He smiled. "Not in the way you understand. Here, economic prosperity flourishes, but material greed has long since faded. Wealth is not hoarded—it is distributed fairly, ensuring that every citizen has what they need to, not only thrive, but also contribute. Not because of enforcement, but because no one desires otherwise. When a society is spiritually mature, selfish ambition dissolves into something far greater—shared progress."

I exhaled, then drew a deeper breath. The momentary silence gave me time to appreciate the magnitude of such an evolved society.

"And education? What do you even teach in a world like this?"

Landorf's expression warmed. "Everything. Knowledge, wisdom, creativity—these are the pursuits of every citizen. Education never ends, because there is always more to learn. We seek understanding not just of our world, but of the universe itself. Art, philosophy, science, and spiritual truth are woven together into a single path of discovery. When people no longer struggle to survive, they turn their energy toward enlightenment."

Landorf gently added, "And when survival is no longer in question, each day becomes a celebration—of life, creation, and exploration. On Avona, happiness isn't pursued; it is lived."

He paused, as if making sure I had fully grasped the importance of what he was sharing before continuing.

"Here, the highest pursuit isn't wealth or status—it's discovery."

Landorf's gaze held something deeper—a reverence for what had been built. "The highest honors are bestowed upon our philosophers," he declared. "Next, our leaders are recognized—not for power, but for service, for their unwavering loyalty to the public's trust."

Then, with quiet certainty, he turned to me. "This is where Vanatta and I come in. As planetary ambassadors, we guide evolving worlds as they approach the threshold of Light and Life."

I blinked, remembering Deja once mentioning *'The Great Teachers.'* I wondered, were Landorf and Vanatta the teachers she was referring to?

"Then why not Earth?

Landorf smiled, knowing that would be my next question. "Because your world is not yet ready," he answered, his tone, apologetic.

I exhaled. I wasn't surprised, but still, hearing it stated so plainly stung.

"How so?"

He clasped his hands behind his back, taking a few measured steps before answering. "Ah, yes… well, it is the duty of every world to begin the journey on its own free will—to find the path and follow it without intervention. No civilization can be handed enlightenment; it must be sought, discovered, and earned. Your world, though it has begun searching, has yet to truly recognize and agree upon the path."

I frowned. "So, we're on our own?"

"Not entirely—unseen forces are always at work. As for direct, otherworld guidance—it will come only when your world has cultivated a harmony of spirit and mind sufficient to receive such presence. Without a foundation of shared values and spiritual clarity, our presence would risk sowing confusion rather than fostering light. We come only when the heart of a world is ready—not to lead, but to walk beside."

His voice remained gentle, but there was a weight behind his words. I let out a slow breath, rubbing the back of my neck.

"Well, if that's the case, we might be waiting a while."

Landorf remained silent, letting the weight of my own words settle. The thought left me uneasy. What would it take for my world to reach that point?

My arms dropped to my side, my voice quieter now. "How do we know when a world is ready?"

Landorf's gaze swept across the tranquil landscape before settling back on me. "When an evolutionary world approaches the threshold of Light and Life, the signs are unmistakable.

"War, as a means of resolving conflict, has faded into history—replaced by diplomacy. Governments are stabilizing, operating with wisdom and justice rather than greed and ambition. While remnants of materialism, nationalism, and inequality may linger, progress is accelerating, and the collective consciousness shifts toward unity. Scientific and technological advances are serving the greater good, and the public has begun to embrace its place in the cosmic family.

"Crime and poverty have nearly vanished—not by force, but by transformation. In a society illuminated by spirit, such shadows no longer find a place to take root. A spiritually enlightened society does not produce individuals who harm one another."

I swallowed hard, trying to picture it. A world without war? Without corruption, greed, or violence? The concept was almost alien.

I wanted to believe it. But the Earth I knew was dominated by governments fueled by self-interest; laws bent by wealth and power; wars fought over land, ideology, and ego.

Landorf spoke of a future that felt as distant as the stars above us.

I exhaled sharply. "That sounds like a dream."

"So did flight to a man who had never left the ground," he replied softly.

I had no response. He was right. People once thought it impossible to fly—until one day, it wasn't.

Was Earth's transformation inevitable—or was it waiting on someone to believe it could be?"

And—was it my responsibility to help make it happen?

The very thought made me break out in a sweat for the first time since arriving on Avona.

I drew a slow breath, but it didn't help. Who was I to take on such an impossible task? But then again… seeing Avona's peace, could I possibly turn away?

My mind churned, spiraling between disbelief and inevitability. The idea of Earth reaching such a transformation felt... impossible. And yet, standing here, how could I deny what I was seeing?

Without another word, our attention turned back to the illuminated Avonian landscape—the flawless balance, the effortless beauty, the quiet serenity that hummed in the very air, just as one might expect of a world at peace. This isn't just an advanced civilization... it's something entirely different. Something I can barely even comprehend.

I turned back to Landorf, my voice only slightly above a whisper. "So... this is what happens when a world gets it right?"

He nodded. "Yes, Patrick. This is what happens when a world chooses, again and again, to walk in the direction of Light. Not once, not in a moment—but across generations, until the path becomes the culture."

And in that moment, I was no longer just listening—I was committed. Earth didn't have to stay trapped in cycles of conflict, scarcity, and fear. I could see it now. Not only was change possible—it felt urgent, even necessary.

I turned back toward the breathtaking view of Pardysia, birdsong drifting through the fragrant air, the quiet hum of serenity settling into me like a bliss so full it left no room for doubt. And I realized something unexpected—that the work of changing a world begins not in governments or movements, but in the convictions of just one soul, willing to try.

All I had to do now was learn what it takes to get there.
And I wasn't leaving Avona until I did.

Chapter 11

Sanctifying Values

I took a deep breath and let it all out. "Tell me, Landorf… what was the deciding factor? The tipping point that set your society on the right path?"

Landorf's expression held something close to satisfaction, as though he'd been waiting for me to ask this very question. His smile was knowing, his pause deliberate. Then, locking eyes with me, his gaze sharp and unwavering, he finally answered.

"We sanctified our supreme values."

"Huh?" I frowned, shifting my weight. "Sanctified?"

Landorf nodded. "Yes."

I let out a breath, running a hand through my hair. "That's it?" I asked, unable to hide my disappointment. "You're going to have to do better than that, Landorf."

His smile deepened—not amused, just patient. "No Patrick. That is everything. Every social decision begins with a single question: *Is it sustainable?* And the supreme values predict the outcomes."

Every cell in me was listening.

"There are seven supreme values," he stated, voice steady, "etched into the very DNA of humanity by The Creator. They exist on every inhabited world, in every galaxy, guiding the course of civilization whether people recognize them or not."

Landorf paused, meeting my gaze, checking to see if I truly understood the significance of what he was teaching me.

"From the very beginning, these values unconsciously shape human progress. Yet until they are understood and applied consciously, civilizations rise and fall, flourish and collapse—repeating the same cycles over and over."

He let that settle before adding, "Think of all the great empires that once stood on your world—now nothing more than remnants. Why are they gone? What caused them to fall?"

I exhaled, shaking my head. "Does anyone really know?"

"When your people finally learn the answer," he instructed, "you'll have taken the first step toward building a society that can endure—not just for centuries, but for the ages."

I studied his face. "Are you going to tell me?"

He didn't answer right away. Instead, he turned back toward the edge of the garden and crouched beside a delicate bloom, cradling its stem between his fingers. The silence stretched between us, deliberate, almost expectant.

I followed his gaze, drawn to the flower. It was breathtaking—deep crimson petals fading into pristine white at the edges, each layer ruffled like the folds of fine silk. The variegation of color, the way the red bled into the white, made it look almost painted, as if nature itself had taken a brush to it.

Finally, I gave in, nodding toward the flower which looked like a carnation. "What is it?"

"A carnation," he affirmed, glancing up at me. "You have these on your planet, don't you?"

I chuckled, "Yeah… we sure do."

As I said it, something about the conversation struck me—this wasn't the first time I'd noticed parallels between Earth and Avona.

The longer I was here, the more I saw it. Was it just coincidence? Or something more?

"Do you actually call them carnations?" I asked.

"No," he responded with a small smile. "Here, we call them gemdosiahs. But they are essentially the same—Flowers of the Gods, symbols of love, and a garnish for culinary delights on your planet. Of all the varieties, this is my favorite."

He brushed his finger along the petals. "I'm partial to hues of red. They signify love and affection here just as they do on your world. Some things, it seems, are universal."

I watched him for a moment, then asked, "How long before you think we'll catch up?"

Landorf didn't acknowledge the question. Instead, he straightened, meeting my gaze.

"Patrick, the supreme values are the path that must be discovered before a society can hope to sustain itself. They are there, waiting. Obvious when pointed out. But when given freely, they are easily ignored—or worse, forgotten."

He let the words linger, then added, "Only when they are consciously realized and then socially sanctified can they serve as the foundation of a lasting civilization."

His voice carried a quiet finality, a certainty that made my stomach tighten.

I swallowed. "You're saying they're that important?"

"I'm saying they are everything."

The words hit with the force of a gavel.

Landorf held my gaze, his expression unwavering. "No civilization can endure without them."

The silence between us stretched, pressing down like gravity.

Then, with a quiet breath, he sealed the thought like a fate already decided.

"And Patrick… it is the reason your current societies will also fail."

My breath felt tight in my chest. I wanted to argue. To push back. To prove Landorf wrong.

But... how could I?

He was right. The great empires of Earth had fallen. Every single one.

It wasn't hard to guess who would be next.

I pondered the irony of it—I'd come to Avona to learn how to make Earth better, and here was Landorf, telling me that our societies were doomed to fail.

But before I could sink too deeply into that thought, he smiled— that benevolent, compassionate smile of his. It was silent encouragement to move forward. So, I did.

"And these values..." I groaned, rolling my eyes dramatically. "You're going to make me work for them, aren't you?"

Landorf's expression held no surprise. "What we work for, we value more deeply. That is simply human nature. Whether Earthling or Avonian, wisdom must be earned. It can't be borrowed, Patrick. And if it's given too freely, it's rarely kept."

As he spoke, he idly trimmed the lower leaves from the gemdosiahs beside him, his movements precise yet unconscious, as if tending to the flowers was as natural as breathing.

"It's the experience of finding them," he continued, inspecting a bloom before moving to the next. "That is what makes the difference."

I sighed, watching him work as my mind turned over his words. What could these values be?

Landorf's voice pulled me back. "Purely bestowed wisdom is only rented, Patrick. You don't own it, because you lack the experience of acquiring it." He paused, snipping off a spent blossom before meeting my gaze. "It is the process of gaining wisdom that makes it permanent."

I exhaled sharply. "So, what you're saying is, it's the journey—not just the knowledge itself—that makes the difference?"

He gave a slow nod. "Exactly."

I wasn't about to let this go. "Landorf, I don't want to leave here without understanding this. Please, tell me—what are the supreme values?"

His answer was immediate. "You already know them."

I groaned. "You won't tell me?"

"I will not," he said with a patient smile, "but I will help you find them."

I gave him a long, sideways look before sighing. "So, we're going to play a game?"

Landorf chuckled. "If you'd like to call it that, then yes."

His gaze flickered toward the city below. Then, turning back to me, he posed a question.

"Tell me, Patrick—what is the most fundamental thing required to exist? And don't overthink it. The answer is simple."

I frowned. "Uh… air? Food?"

Landorf's expression didn't change. "More basic than that."

I hesitated, turning the question over in my mind. More basic? What could be more basic than air, food, water?

Then, the answer hit me.

"Life."

As soon as I said it, a memory surfaced. Vanatta. I heard her voice in my mind:

"…those who value life seek to nurture it, to build, to contribute. Those who do not value life—who prey upon others without conscience—become a destabilizing force."

I straightened. "Life! That has to be the first value. Without life, nothing else matters."

Landorf's face broke into a pleased smile, like a teacher watching their student have a breakthrough.

"Yes, Patrick. *Life* is the most supreme of all the supreme values."

I thought about that. It made sense.

I remembered the times I had helped a giant cane spider escape my beach shack rather than kill it. The way I marveled at anything alive, thinking to myself, *I could never make one of these*, so what right do I have to destroy it?

Landorf's eyes gleamed, as if reading my thoughts.

"You see, Patrick, this is the natural instinct of most humans—to protect and honor life. But there are others…" He paused, his expression darkening, eyes closing briefly as if recalling tragedies long past. "There are those who take life without a second thought, who kill not out of necessity, but for pleasure or personal gain. Those who, like animals, value only their own survival."

I nodded grimly. I'd seen it firsthand.

Landorf continued. "On Avona, disregard for life is recognized as an inhuman trait. It is one of the social metrics by which we identify predators. Long ago our society made the conscious decision to sanctify life as the highest value—a guiding principle by which all decisions, all choices must be measured."

He looked at me seriously. "When something—anything—violates, prevents, or interferes with *Life*, we recognize it for what it is—an obstacle to social sustainability. And as such, it cannot be allowed to coexist within our society."

A strange thought occurred. "Does that mean nobody kills bugs?"

Landorf chuckled. "It means that every world must bring its environment into balance. We do not kill mindlessly, but we do take necessary action when a species becomes invasive or dangerous."

I exhaled. "So, basically, if Vanatta stepped on a cockroach, it wouldn't be a crime?"

Landorf let out a patient sigh, shaking his head with amusement. "Patrick… I think you already know the answer."

I smirked. "Just making sure."

Landorf studied me for a long moment. Then, with quiet certainty, he asked:

"So, you have one value. Care to try for another?"

"Trust," I blurted out, sure I'd nailed it.

"Close, but not supreme."

I blinked. "Wait—how is trust not a supreme value?" I asked, incredulously. "Didn't you say your leaders' *'unwavering loyalty to the public's trust'* was essential for a stable society?"

"Trust is a derivative," Landorf explained patiently. "It springs from a value that is supreme—one that must be present before trust can be established. Tell me, Patrick, when you buy something on your planet, how much do you expect to pay for it?"

I frowned. "I don't know… a fair price, I guess?"

"Exactly. And why a fair price? What makes it fair?"

"Well… I guess both parties should feel like they benefit equally."

Landorf nodded. "Now imagine that principle applied to every transaction, of every kind, everywhere. Imagine if *'both parties feeling equally benefited'* was the standard, an expectation so ingrained that no one even questioned it. What would that do to trust?"

I exhaled, the answer dawning on me. "Trust would become automatic."

"Precisely. So, what is the value that creates the conditions for trust?"

Duh. It hit me like a freight train.

"**Equality**," I declared. The light bulb flicked on, and I remembered—Landorf had said it before. That *"a moral society provides every citizen with an equal opportunity to realize their full potential."* I should have remembered.

Landorf smiled, reading my thoughts. "Yes, you should have. But you didn't, because it wasn't earned. Now, you just might never forget it."

His grin was triumphant, and I found myself mirroring it.

"So how do you use equality as a metric?" I asked.

Landorf's expression turned thoughtful. "You have private schools on your planet, yes?"

"Yeah… why?"

"We don't," he stated simply.

I raised a brow. "No private schools? Why not?"

"Because they fail the *equal access to opportunity* test. If one education system is superior to another, those who attend it will become smarter, richer, better connected, and more privileged than the rest. A class system forms—an inequality that separates people. And separation is the antithesis of sustainability."

I let that sink in. "So… you don't even let the system exist?"

"That's right," he confirmed. "We don't waste time or resources on models we already know will fail in the long run. The moment we identify something as unequal, we recognize the instability it will create and prevent it from taking root."

I thought about private schools back home—the wealthy parents who funded them, the kids who attended them, the cycle of privilege that never ended.

"I think the rich people on my planet would hate sending their kids to public school," I muttered.

"If private schools didn't exist," Landorf countered, "the wealthy would have no choice but to invest in everyone's education—because their children would be part of the same system. Their self-interest would align with societal interest."

"Duh. Of course it would. If they had no other choice, they'd have to make public education great."

"And because education is one of the most crucial factors in a sustainable society," Landorf added, "this example perfectly illustrates how the supreme value of equality can—and must—be applied."

I nodded enthusiastically, the concept clicking into place. "Okay, as long as there's no homework—I hate homework."

Landorf chuckled. "Fortunately, in a society that values equality, education is designed to be engaging, not punishing."

I smirked. "I'll believe it when I see it."

Still, the idea made sense. Maybe there was hope for Earth after all.

A wave of optimism lightened my mood. Without thinking, I lowered myself onto the garden path and sat beside Landorf, resting an arm on my knee as he continued tending his flowers.

"Alright," I sighed, running a finger along the intricate patterns of the mosaic path beneath me. "We've identified *Life* and *Equality* as supreme values. What's next?"

Landorf's smile widened. "You tell me, Patrick. You're on a roll."

I hesitated. "We've already discussed them all, haven't we?"

He nodded. "You know them. I've given them to you before—but now, because you must work to retrieve them, they will stay with you."

I furrowed my brow, rifling through our past conversations. I did remember everything—I had total recall of every discussion—but I hadn't been thinking in terms of supreme values.

Landorf studied me, then asked, "Patrick, why did you come here?"

I blinked. "What?"

"To Avona. Why are you here?"

"Uh… I asked Deja what life was like on other planets?"

"Yes. And why did you ask?"

"I guess I was curious?"

"All right," Landorf inquired. "Is everyone you know curious about life on other planets?"

"Well… maybe? I don't know. I just wanted to learn—" I stopped mid-sentence, realization creeping in. "I wanted to learn. I wanted to know how we could solve our problems on Earth… I wanted insight into how others had done it."

Landorf's eyes sparkled. "But you didn't *need* to know. You could have gone about your life, never asking, never wondering. Why do you want to know?"

I exhaled, feeling the answer forming before I spoke. "Because I want to learn. I have a passion for understanding. I want to know how things work, why things fail, how things can improve. I want to grow."

Landorf's lips curled into a knowing smile.

"Bingo."

I blinked. "Wait… what?" How does Landorf know about bingo? Then it hit me.

"Growth."

"Yes," he said, pleased. "Whatever does not grow, stagnates. And stagnation is death. Individuals must grow. Societies must grow. If they do not, they collapse."

He gestured toward the city below.

"Institutions, governments, economies—without growth, they become brittle and eventually crumble. This is simple social math. Growth is not an option, Patrick. It is a requirement."

I nodded slowly. *Life, Equality,* and *Growth.* It was becoming clearer.

And then, as if the next realization had been lying in wait, it struck me.

"That explains why Avona has such a high quality of life…"

Landorf's smile widened.

"And there's your next value," he beamed.

I frowned. "Wait, what?"

"Patrick, stop overthinking this," he gently scolded, shaking his head. "The supreme values are not hidden. They are woven into your DNA. They already guide normal humans instinctively. The only difference is whether they are unconscious—or recognized and sanctified."

I felt the pieces snapping into place.

"Quality of Life," I breathed. "That's the fourth value, isn't it? "

"Yes it is," Landorf confirmed, his voice quiet but full of conviction. "Every normal human seeks to improve their quality of life, whether consciously or subconsciously. It is the driving force behind almost every decision."

I exhaled, shaking my head.

Life. Equality. Growth. Quality of Life.

I had uncovered four.

It seemed so simple yet made so much sense. Too much sense. I wanted to know more.

Landorf let the moment stretch before speaking again, his hands absently tending to his flowers. "When Life, Equality, and Growth are upheld as supreme values, the individual's Quality of Life is naturally enhanced. And as such, society follows suit."

I rubbed my chin, considering that. "So, you're saying that society reaches *settled status* as a natural result of its citizens recognizing these values?"

"Almost." Landorf, continuing to trim lower leaves from the gemdosiah stems. "First, the supreme values must be recognized. Then, they must be sanctified—formally accepted as the standards by which every choice, every action, every policy is measured.

"Only then can society fully align itself. When the people embody the values, the world follows. Not the other way around."

He said it so casually, so matter-of-fact, as if he were explaining how to boil water. But the weight of his words landed with an impact I couldn't ignore.

"Society is what its citizens become," he continued. "Not the reverse. As the people evolve, so does the world they shape. Society can never exceed the moral and intellectual capacity of the individuals who comprise it."

I exhaled. "So… if the foundation is flawed, the building collapses."

Landorf nodded. "That's right."

He straightened, brushing soil from his hands. "Your material sciences have long surpassed your social sciences. You have physics, chemistry, mathematics—all built upon established, agreed-upon principles. But your world still hasn't built a framework for social sustainability."

"So, you're saying we need a universal metric for society? Like, a set of rules as solid as math?"

Landorf's lips twitched into a smile. "Social math is *very real*, Patrick. There are cause-and-effect laws that determine whether a civilization thrives or collapses. These principles are immutable—whether they are recognized, agreed upon, or even believed."

He gestured toward me. "You already understand one example. A society cannot sustain itself while tolerating unchecked, antisocial behavior—those who exploit, manipulate, or harm others without a flicker of conscience. If such predators go unrestrained, society deteriorates."

I nodded slowly.

"The same is true for equality," he continued. "If some people are granted more access to opportunity than others, instability is inevitable. Those denied the opportunity to develop their full potential will eventually rise in resistance—whether through protest, rebellion, or collapse. It is foreseeable.

He turned away from his flowers for a moment to face me, as if to emphasize his point. "Just like gravity, inequality pulls civilizations downward. It's as predictable as physics—ignore it, and the collapse isn't a matter of if, but when. That's social math."

I rubbed the back of my neck. "And yet… we still keep making the same mistakes."

Landorf chuckled softly. "Because you choose to ignore the underlying causes. You cannot solve an equation if you refuse to acknowledge the numbers."

I let that sink in, and then suddenly I saw what Earth was lacking—not just the absence of peace, but the absence of pattern. Our world wasn't failing because we were flawed; it was failing because we lacked the framework upon which to build our systems. Avona has structure—a living architecture of sustainability, a way of weighing decisions before they're acted upon;. All we have is noise. This wasn't just abstract philosophy. It was tangible—measurable.

Was I meant to carry this truth home? The thought made my chest tighten—not with fear, but with the weight of responsibility.

I took a slow breath, turning my gaze to the distant city below. "Landorf… you said there are seven values. What are the other three?"

Landorf grinned, turning back to his flowers. "The next one is close. You've circled around it already—several times."

I groaned, rubbing my temples. "So, we're still playing the game?"

"Until you win," he quipped, with amusing calm.

Chapter 12

The Price of Peace

I pushed off from the garden path, brushing stray petals from my palms. Landorf rose effortlessly beside me. He gestured toward a winding path leading uphill, away from the gemdosiahs. Without a word, we began walking.

The garden gave way to a broader, open plateau. Ahead, a grand pavilion stretched before us, its towering, multicolored crystallineum arches filtering the golden midday light. The entire structure seemed to shimmer, refracting beams of color across the smooth mosaic pathways.

I tilted my head, marveling. "Landorf, these arches… they're magnificent! Are all of those crystals?"

"They are," he replied.

"The colors… there are so many." I scanned the dazzling array—reds and yellows, greens and blues, white and violet—woven into intricate patterns so precise they felt divinely inspired.

At the heart of the pavilion, a large reflecting pond glowed with an inner radiance, its bottom encrusted with gemstones. Handrails of gold curved elegantly into the luminous water. Along the perimeter, colossal monuments stood in solemn tribute to what I presumed to be leaders of Avona's past.

Children's laughter echoed from the distant edges of the plaza, blending with the gentle murmur of Avonians in quiet discussion. Some sat on crystallineum benches, others waded in the shallows of the pond. A few stood motionless, heads bowed in meditation.

A feeling settled over me—something vast, something weighty. I couldn't put words to it, but it pressed against my entire being like the silent push of an unseen current.

Landorf slowed his steps. "This is a place of remembrance."

I turned to him, waiting.

"This is where we honor those who made the hard choices that ushered Avona into the Light."

I caught the shift in his tone—the reverence, the quiet finality.

"And especially," he added, "those who made the most difficult choice of all—the one that finally allowed us to move forward."

Something in my stomach twisted. "The most difficult choice?"

Landorf's expression softened, though his voice carried the weight of history. "The choice no society wishes to face, yet must, to secure its future."

I wasn't sure I liked the sound of that.

He motioned for me to sit. We lowered ourselves onto a deep blue crystallineum bench at the pavilion's edge. A fallen blossom lay beside him, and he idly turned it between his fingers.

The moment stretched between us, filled with the quiet hum of the plaza. Then, without looking up, Landorf asked, "Patrick, have you thought about what the other three supreme values might be?"

I blinked, caught off guard. I had completely lost track of the 'game' we'd been playing. The beauty of the pavilion, the vibrant gardens, the warm golden light of midday—it had all swept me away.

But now Landorf was looking at me, expectant.

I exhaled, shifting in my seat. "What do you suppose makes predators a threat to society?" he asked.

I frowned. "I guess… they don't care about other people. They only care about themselves?"

He was silent, waiting.

I stared toward the reflecting pond. "I suppose the only life they really value is their own, right?"

Landorf's knowing smile told me I was circling something just out of reach.

"And the same applies to growth," I continued. "They pursue their own success, but usually at the expense of others."

Landorf gave an approving nod. "And why do you think that is?"

I rubbed my hands together. "Because they don't care about others."

"Fine," he smirked. "So, what do you call that?"

I hesitated. "…A lack of empathy?"

"That's one," he confirmed. "And what does empathy lead to?"

I thought for a moment. "Compassion?"

"That's two."

I straightened, feeling a rush of clarity. The last missing piece turned over in my mind, and then—just like that—it clicked.

"**Love**. It has to be love. Predators don't love people. That's why they can exploit them without guilt or remorse."

"Yes." Landorf's voice was solemn, but firm.

The silence lingered between us for several minutes as I thought about the connection between the last three values. Feeling a little unsure about the difference between empathy and compassion, I asked Landorf to explain.

He smiled slightly, as though he'd been waiting for the question to surface.

"Patrick, empathy is when you feel what another is feeling—you step into their perspective, share their sorrow or their joy. It's resonance, a recognition. But compassion goes further. Compassion takes that recognition and turns it outward. It is the will to act, to relieve the suffering you've felt through empathy."

He brushed a bit of garden soil from his sleeve and lifted his gaze toward the pond. "Think of it this way: empathy is *feeling with,* while compassion is *acting for*. One arises from perception, the other from choice. Empathy opens the heart; compassion engages the hands."

I nodded slowly, letting the distinction settle into place.

"And love?" I asked quietly.

"Love," he replied, voice low and certain, "is when empathy and compassion become one seamless flow. It is both the feeling and the doing—an orientation of the soul that seeks the good of another as naturally as breathing."

I thought about that for a minute. Then it dawned on me why predators are a social threat—lacking empathy and compassion, they're *unable* to love.

Landorf, always following my thoughts added, "And that is why they must be removed."

The word caught me off guard. *Removed?* …what exactly did he mean? I let out a long breath. I was unsure if I'd heard him correctly, and a little afraid to ask.

"Otherwise," he continued, "society will rise and fall indefinitely, for millennium after millennium.

Silence stretched between us, broken only by the occasional rustle of leaves in the wind.

Then, without looking at me, he gestured toward the trees lining the pavilion's edge. Their branches hung low with ripe, golden fruit, their scent sweet on the breeze.

"Have you heard the saying, Patrick? *One rotten apple spoils the whole barrel.*"

I nodded as he motioned toward a single piece of fruit on the ground, its skin bruised, mottled with patches of soft decay. I took a deep breath, suspecting I knew where this was going.

"When an apple begins to rot, it releases a gas," he continued. "That gas accelerates the decay of the fruit around it. If left unchecked, the rot spreads. Eventually, the entire batch goes bad."

A gentle breeze stirred the trees. Another piece of fruit dropped. We both watched it roll to a stop, the silence stretching again—heavier this time.

"The same is true for society," Landorf added, his voice even. "Predators are not just individual problems. They are accelerants. Left unchecked, they spread their decay. And before long, the core of civilization begins to rot."

I ran a hand down my face and stroked my chin. The analogy was too perfect. Too undeniable.

I thought about our economic predators—those who grow rich by preying on the ignorance of others. Insurance scams, fake charities, pyramid schemes, loan sharks, TV evangelists—all conducting their get rich quick "businesses" with impunity, encouraging others to follow suit.

"That's right." Landorf said, replying to my thought. "Your world has no shortage of those releasing their 'gas' and spreading the rot."

"So," I asked, my voice quieter now, "how? …exactly how do you 'remove' them?"

"We compassionately escort them to the next phase of their soul's journey," he replied, his voice imbued with solemn reverence. "Painlessly. Even mercifully—and without retribution. Not as punishment— but as protection for the whole, *especially* our future generations."

He paused for a moment before further clarifying.

"We do not end a soul. We end their capacity to destabilize the living. What becomes of them beyond this world lies in hands far wiser than ours."

I tensed, pulse thrumming in my ears. I wanted to recoil—but part of me couldn't argue with the results.

Landorf remained composed. If anything, his tone was even more gentle.

"We move them along to the next step of their spiritual journey," he continued. "Their survival after death is a matter of their own choices. Here, we know that mortal death is not final. That divine justice always prevails—determined by the wisdom of The Creator."

I stared at him, not sure whether to be horrified… or strangely relieved.

My gut twisted. Every instinct screamed that it was wrong—yet everything around me said otherwise. How could something that felt so morally troubling create such undeniable peace?

I swallowed hard. This was the most difficult concept for me to accept. Somewhere deep inside, I realized I wasn't fighting the truth—I was fighting the feeling that I might have known it all along.

"Patrick," Landorf's voice softened further, "our choice wasn't made in anger. It was made with sorrow—but also with hope, compassionately understanding our duty to future generations."

I remained speechless. Of all the controversies on my home world, the so-called "death penalty" was one of the most fiercely debated. Yet as Landorf explained it, I sensed no vindictiveness. No thirst for revenge. A decision made, not out of hatred for the predator, but out of love for humanity. An obligation—not just to the present, but to their children, to all future generations.

I looked around at the utopia surrounding me. How could I argue with the results?

Still, I kept my face neutral—even though I knew he was listening to the storm of questions crackling through my mind.
How had they started this process?
Did it happen overnight—or was there a warning?
Who made the decisions?

The thoughts flashed through me all at once, like a single, blinding burst of lightning—brief, but leaving an afterimage burned into my mind. Although I feared the answer, I had to ask.

"Who had that kind of power?"

Landorf met my gaze with quiet resolve. "No one. Not one person *ever* decides. "It didn't happen all at once," he said with measured calm. "Over the course of a hundred years—just four generations—we made the shift. At first, the consequences were lighter, but they grew steadily harsher. Each step was clear, every offense named, so no one could claim they hadn't been warned."

My stomach tightened. "You gave them a warning?"

"A fair one," Landorf nodded. "From the beginning, it was made clear: blatant predation and violations of public trust would no longer be tolerated. By the tenth decade, everyone knew the consequences."

I hesitated. "And then… what happened?"

Landorf's voice remained calm, factual—devoid of drama or cruelty.

"Unsurprisingly, the number of predatory incidents dropped dramatically. Once removal became the consequence, cases of exploitation and corruption nearly disappeared."

He let that settle before adding, "At that point, decisions had already been entrusted to a twelve-member panel of ethicists."

I raised an eyebrow. "A panel of ethicists?"

"Yes," Landorf said. "A select group, prepared not in theory but in practice—trained to weigh justice, truth, and compassion in every choice. Their compass was always the seven supreme values."

I turned that over in my mind before asking, "But what made them qualified?"

He leaned back slightly, his fingers tracing the crystallinum bench. "Many of our citizens studied ethics deeply, learning how to resolve dilemmas with clarity and integrity. From them, only those who proved both wise and steadfast were chosen—never by ambition, always by the measure of our values. They served for a set term, then returned to ordinary life."

I rubbed my chin. "And the decisions… they were always unanimous?"

"Always."

There was weight behind that word.

"Never," he emphasized, "was removal decided by an individual. That would be unethical. Always—*always*—it was a unanimous decision by the governing panel."

I wasn't sure that made me feel better.

He continued, his voice gentle yet unwavering. "The act was always carried out compassionately—even lovingly. Never in retribution, always with the understanding that we were guiding a soul onward, while shaping the future of our society. The decision was never made lightly."

I stared straight ahead. I didn't know *what* to feel. Comforted? …or appalled?

Landorf paused, then gestured out toward the horizon. "From that point forward, our civilization progressed steadily toward social sustainability. Within three hundred years, we had reached the threshold of Light. And today, more than 10,000 years later, we continue to evolve in peace as a *settled* world in the local universe of inhabited planets."

I let out a slow breath. "Whoa! …three hundred years?"

"Yes, Landorf smiled. "Only twenty seconds on Deja's timeline of human history."

I tried to imagine three hundred years into the future on my world. Landorf continued, his gaze sweeping across the vast city in the distance.

"No more war. No more exploitation—economic, industrial, or environmental. No corruption. No violence. No deception. No coercion.

"We feel safe. We trust one another—our institutions, our educators, our leaders.

"And above all, we know that every citizen has equal access to the opportunity to realize their full potential. That's what makes our society great. After all, *you cannot have a great society without great people.* It's… social math."

It had never occurred to me that social choices could follow a formula—what Landorf kept calling *social math.* But it was beginning to make sense. Why shouldn't there be social constants, as fixed and real as mathematical ones? Avona seemed to prove they existed, though Earth had yet to discover them.

I stared at him, then at the tranquil world around me. A world without locks. Without gates. Without police. Without armies, weapons, or prisons. Immediately, I saw how much Earth's resources were wasted on security, barriers, and endless layers of protection.

How much more would be available—how much human potential could be unlocked—if we didn't have to constantly defend ourselves from ourselves?

The realization was almost too much. I felt... *hopeful*. And at the same time, utterly defeated by my perceived impossibility of it all.

I turned back to Landorf, the words bursting out before I could stop them.

"But... what you're describing could never happen on Earth. Where I come from, the death penalty is one of the most bitterly debated issues we have. People fight over it endlessly. Many see it as barbaric. Most believe the 'compassionate' alternative is imprisonment."

Landorf gave a slow nod, as though he had been waiting for this objection. His voice remained calm, but there was an edge of gravity in it.

"Patrick, your world's death penalty is not what we speak of here. Yours is rooted in vengeance. It is administered by juries untrained in ethics, decided through processes riddled with error and prejudice. Too often, the innocent are condemned while the guilty slip free. There is no compassion in that, only retribution. It is no wonder so many oppose it."

I exhaled, my thoughts a whirlwind of contradiction. Landorf leaned forward slightly, meeting my gaze.

"Your societies, your cultures, your humanity—are still evolving. Your destiny is certain, Patrick. Only the timing remains unknown."

I furrowed my brow. "Meaning...?"

"There will come a time when this choice becomes necessary. When humanity must finally decide."

His voice was calm, but I felt the gravity behind it. "And eventually, just as we did… your world will come to understand the price of peace.

"And when it chooses, Patrick, it must choose in Love.

"For the innocent.

"For the future.

"For the wholeness of all."

Chapter 13

The River of Culture

Quietly I sat at the edge of the reflecting pond, my feet dangling mindlessly in its cool, clear water. Landorf's words lingered vividly in my mind, their weight pressing against the serenity around me—daring me to pretend I wasn't overwhelmed.

How could I possibly explain Avona's truths without sounding naive—or worse, unhinged?

Landorf had returned to his gardening project, leaving me gratefully alone to process the myriad concerns I had about the weighty ideas he planted in my head. I remembered back to K-Bay, when Deja invited me to *drink from the fountain of knowledge.* I wasn't sure I'd made the right choice—the 'drink' tasting so bittersweet.

The solitude was comforting—I needed this space to gather my thoughts as Landorf's words echoed within like a tolling bell.

Time slipped by, unmetered. I drifted deeper into the stillness, quietly observing the wrestling match in my head—old notions grappling with new truths, all of it battered by the reality of my world's unreadiness… yet soothed by the unshakable serenity of Avona's settled grace.

In the background, I was vaguely aware of people moving through the courtyard—soft voices blending with rustling leaves and the gentle burble of the pond. If a more peaceful place existed anywhere in the universe, I couldn't imagine it.

So lost in thought, I barely noticed the shadow stretching across the water before me. "Mind if I join you?"

Vanatta's voice broke gently through my reflections.

I glanced up, startled. I hadn't heard her approach. Her serene expression quickly calmed my surprise, her eyes radiating warmth and understanding.

"Please," I answered, smiling and motioning to the spot beside me at the pond's edge. She slipped gracefully out of her sandals, settling comfortably next to me, her feet gently disturbing the water's tranquil surface alongside mine.

For a long moment, neither of us spoke, allowing the courtyard's sacred tranquility to enfold us. My mind inevitably drifted back toward Earth, troubled by the complexities involved in initiating profound societal transformation. Where could we possibly begin?

"Parents," Vanatta said softly.

"Parents?" I repeated, momentarily forgetting she could follow my thoughts.

"Yes, parents," she affirmed gently. "That's your answer. You begin by training parents to become effective and wise—to guide their children with compassion, empathy, and love. Lead parents to discover the seven supreme values, using them as the standard for measuring every aspect of their lives. By doing so, these parents raise children who become wise and effective parents themselves."

She paused, smiling softly. "It's parents. That's where you start."

On Earth we often say, *"children are our future,"* and while that's true, I suddenly realized it overlooked something fundamental—what if these children, who supposedly are our future, lacked the skills to raise their own children well?

Vanatta's voice gently interrupted my internal questioning. "Is the answer not obvious?"

I chuckled lightly. It seemed almost too simple because it *was* so obvious. "Okay, so what's the first step to training these parents?"

"Beliefs and expectations."

I blinked. "Beliefs and expectations?"

"Yes," she explained. "Beliefs and expectations form the root of all disagreements. Differing beliefs, differing expectations—these are at the heart of nearly every conflict. Resolving disagreements is a matter of aligning beliefs and expectations."

I let that thought sink in; it felt undeniably true, and surprisingly straightforward.

She continued, "When people share the same beliefs and expectations, disagreements cease. But when their beliefs are erroneous or their expectations unrealistic, the resulting conflicts lead to disappointment. Conflict with truth inevitably yields disappointing outcomes."

"So how do we avoid that?"

"You peel away the layers," she replied. "Find out why people hold the beliefs they do, then gently guide them to 'discover' truths for themselves..."

"...which leads to realistic expectations," I finished for her. "Fewer disappointments."

"That right," she spoke softly, almost solemnly. "When false beliefs are replaced by truths, people naturally share common expectations. Once everyone measures their decisions using the same social metric— the supreme values—you can solve virtually any misunderstanding."

"And that's how you approach parenting?"

"Yes." She paused and smiled warmly, as if remembering something from a personal experience, perhaps seeing firsthand how transformative these simple truths can be.

I couldn't help but wonder about the actual process. Right on cue, Vanatta answer my thought.

"On Avona, we began by cataloging the beliefs and expectations regarding child rearing of every potential parent. Our catalog became extensive, covering discipline, education, responsibilities, permissions—every imaginable topic and many more beyond. We brought these beliefs and expectations out into the open, evaluated them, identified common ground, and compared them to working models—thus creating a repository of successful techniques.

"Within a few generations, we determined the methods that consistently produced the best outcomes. We formalized this knowledge within our family structures, refining the process continuously and evolving it naturally over time."

I found myself nodding thoughtfully. Families, child-rearing—transforming parenting into an exact science. It made too much sense not to be true.

"So," I asked, "that's the strategy that set your society on the path toward your current utopia?"

"It is," Vanatta replied. "But remember, without the seven supreme values guiding our decisions, it would have been pointless. Only when we embraced the sanctity of these values could families become the channels through which the river of culture and knowledge flowed seamlessly from one generation to the next."

What she was saying reminded me of Landorf's words—that any society ignoring these supreme values was doomed to collapse. Vanatta's approach seemed like a crucial step toward avoiding that outcome.

"So by training citizens to become exceptional parents," I thought aloud, "you're really securing the future by strengthening the very foundation of society—its families."

"Yes." Vanatta's expression warmed as she elaborated. "Within just a few generations, we began raising children who, by example, knew how to become wise, empathetic parents themselves. And so, our virtuous cycle began."

Her voice softened with conviction.

"Today on Avona, parenting schools are compulsory for everyone. Our methodologies remain transparent—always evolving, always open to refinement. This reflects our commitment to the supreme value of Growth."

She paused, thoughtful. "Because parenting became central to our societal vision, we dedicate immense resources to effective child-rearing. At this point, it would be difficult to find any parenting issue that hasn't been encountered, documented, and addressed.

"The result is a vast, living library of ever-improving guidelines—freely accessible to all."

I hesitated, then admitted, "Honestly, Vanatta… it sounds incredible—at least in theory. But I'm still unclear on one thing: how did you actually get started?"

She smiled patiently, anticipating my question. "Like your planet, we had to begin somewhere. Our starting point was identifying families that had successfully raised productive, well-adjusted, and happy children. We interviewed these families extensively, noting which parenting techniques they employed. We analyzed and distilled our data, correlating common elements into actionable guidelines.

"Crucially," she added, "we only studied the positive outcomes. We didn't waste time on what didn't work. We discovered that, by nurturing effective practices, the negative methods naturally faded away.

"Within a single generation, we had our initial guidelines. Ever since, we've been refining our processes—for centuries."

Vanatta paused when she sensed I had another question. "You're saying you never studied the cases that went wrong—the individuals who turned out poorly?"

"That's correct. We focused exclusively on citizens who matured into responsible, contributing adults, carefully analyzing the parenting techniques that shaped them. There was no need to waste energy studying what clearly failed. We dedicated our brightest minds, our philosophers, our resources solely to understanding what succeeded."

She let that rest for a few minutes to allow me to process these ideas. Once I had caught up, she added, "We recognized there was something you might call 'social math.'"

"Social math," I repeated, recalling that Landorf had explained that concept earlier.

"Yes—cause-and-effect relationships that are constants in society."

Sensing that I wanted an example, Vanatta elaborated, "If parents have no training, how can they possibly know optimal child-rearing methods?"

The question seemed rhetorical, but I answered anyway. "I guess they can't."

"That's right," she continued gently. "And without that training, they're prone to poor decisions. They unknowingly pass these inadequate methods to their children, who in turn repeat their parents' mistakes, generation after generation."

She paused briefly, allowing the significance of her point to resonate. "On one level, this failure is immediate: poorly trained children are unprepared for the responsibilities of citizenship."

"Okay, that makes sense."

"But on another level," she pressed further, "these same children are ill-equipped to raise their own children properly, perpetuating this failure indefinitely. Eventually, a society collapses because its citizens never learned how to maintain it. When too many individuals cannot fulfill roles that uplift society, they inevitably become burdens—it's simple social math. The outcome is foreseeable from the very beginning."

"Okay," I finally muttered, trying to shake off my pessimism. "So, how do we break this cycle?"

Vanatta considered for a moment, clearly sensing my need for a tangible starting point.

"Enclaves," she said simply.

I glanced sideways, "Excuse me?"

"Enclaves," she repeated patiently. "Given your world's current state, one effective way forward is to build enclaves of awareness—small communities that start with a few committed individuals who sanctify the seven supreme values and choose to live by them. When these communities lead by example, their results do the convincing. Others notice, become curious, and desire similar outcomes. This organic growth is key."

"Like the Amish communities on Earth?" I asked skeptically.

"Similar, but not necessarily by rejecting technology. What's important isn't isolation, but creating communities whose members consciously choose ethical living. They don't hide from evil; they learn how to confront it effectively as it arises. Most importantly, they teach their children ethical and moral living, showing them how to attract good into their lives."

"Is that the only way?" I pressed.

"No, Patrick. But it's one possibility. When a world experiences confusion and chaos on the level that yours does now, creating ethical enclaves can act as incubators—safe spaces to nurture and protect these values."

I could tell she sensed my skepticism. I wondered how such groups could withstand the influence of the outside world? On cue, Vanatta continued.

"Of course, such communities will face challenges. But over time, their strength—rooted in shared values—makes them resilient. The like-minded groups begin to merge, grow stronger, and eventually reshape the wider culture. Ethical behavior becomes the norm. Predatory behaviors, by contrast, often self-destruct—undone by their own competitive instability. Then, as value-based ethics become the norm, they begin to fade away. At which point, your society can begin compassionately addressing and removing the remaining predators."

Although I listened closely, I was uneasy. I struggled to imagine how it could actually work. Vanatta, sensing my doubt, continued gently.

"Patrick, I'm talking about groups of people—be it fifty, five hundred, or even millions—individuals deeply dedicated to equality and growth. Communities where life itself is revered, and the highest quality of life is prioritized for everyone. Communities founded on compassion, empathy, and love for humanity. You doubt their potential because you underestimate what committed people can achieve."

"Would these enclaves govern themselves?"

"Governance should reflect the needs and capacities of the community. Initially, complete self-governance might not be practical. Often, a deliberative council—non-authoritative yet respected—can provide recommendations and guidance for equitable living."

I shifted uncomfortably. "This is beginning to sound like communism."

"Not at all," she shook her head gently. "Human nature craves personal possessions... your own world's attempts at communal living often failed precisely because they disregarded human ambition rather than channeling it constructively.

"Communism fundamentally inhibits individual growth, making it unsustainable. A truly sustainable society recognizes ambition and accommodates individual striving—but ensures profit is never exploitive or achieved at the expense of others. All parties must benefit equally.

"And what about democracy?"

She paused thoughtfully. "Democracy is admirable, perhaps even ideal—but it presumes an educated, informed citizenry. Until that citizenry intellectually matures, it's wise—even necessary—to be governed by an ethically qualified council. Such leadership must be accountable and, above all, adhere unwaveringly to the seven supreme values.

"The precise structure or ideological label doesn't matter nearly as much as integrity and adaptability. A functional society's institutions must continuously evolve to meet changing circumstances and needs."

I thought of my own country—still governed by a constitution written more than two centuries ago. We treat it like scripture, endlessly trying to force its old framework to fit modern realities. Like hammering a square peg into a round hole.

Vanatta's wide smile and quiet chuckle reminded me again that she was following my thoughts. "Trying to fit a square peg into a round hole" she repeated, obviously amused.

I nodded.

She chuckled. "With enough force, I suppose you could make it fit. But you'd ruin the peg—and the hole."

I laughed, picturing the splinters. "Wouldn't it be easier to just find a round peg?"

"Much," she grinned, still amused by the image of our battered tools and stubborn traditions.

I swirled my feet in the cool water as we sat in thoughtful silence. Eventually, curiosity prompted me to ask, "How did Avona begin this process? Were enclaves your starting point?"

"Our situation differed somewhat. Our ethical age preceded our technological one. By the time our technology reached a stage capable of global impact, we had already eliminated social predation. Your world, however, is reversed. You've developed advanced technology first—and unfortunately, that amplifies predatory power exponentially."

My mind raced immediately to nuclear weapons and the vast military-industrial complex born after World War II.

Vanatta continued, her voice calm yet earnest. "And that is why your world urgently needs to address predation. Technology itself isn't the issue; the ethical vacuum that enables its misuse is the real danger. Predators exploit power unchecked. And they succeed because your ethical foundation is missing the—"

"—seven supreme values," I muttered sadly as Vanatta nodded sympathetically.

A heavy sigh escaped me as the gravity of Earth's predicament weighed heavily on my spirit. Despite the obvious need, I knew that change couldn't happen overnight.

Vanatta, as usual, followed my thoughts closely. "You're right, Patrick. Urgency alone can't accelerate certain universal processes."

"Universal processes?"

"Indeed," she affirmed gently. "There's a universally recognized path for societal evolution. Deviating from it is pointless."

"Recognized by whom?"

"Every enlightened personality across the universe. Once again, it's social math."

I hesitated, prompting her to offer an analogy.

"When baking a cake," she explained patiently, "you must carefully select the correct ingredients and follow precise instructions. Turn up the heat or shorten the baking time to hurry the process, and you'll ruin the cake."

I began to understand. "You're saying building an ethical society is like baking a cake?"

"Yes. People are your ingredients. You must start with the right people—dedicated, aware, compassionate. The supreme values represent your baking temperature—essential, precise, and non-negotiable. Deviating from them risks societal ruin, much like increasing heat would burn your cake."

I nodded thoughtfully. "Then generations must represent baking time."

"Yes," she said gently, almost in a whisper. "Societies, like cakes, cannot be rushed. Both require patience, careful attention, and the right conditions to truly rise."

"But what if we don't have that much time?" I pressed anxiously. "What if Earth's problems are already too critical?"

"They *are* critical," she eagerly agreed, "and your society absolutely should start now. The cake analogy still applies—rushing the process won't help. It may indeed get messy while mixing the ingredients and waiting for it to 'bake,' but delaying the start will only make the process even messier."

The challenges facing Earth felt overwhelming, and I sighed heavily again.

"To achieve sustainability," Vanatta continued, sensing my exhaustion, "you must approach social math backward, starting from your desired outcome."

I raised an eyebrow. "Backward?"

"Correct. Work backwards from the goal—*sustainably constant societal evolution*. For evolution to occur, equity is required, maximizing the contributions of all. Universal equity demands broad access to information and opportunity. Effective use of information and opportunity requires education. Education alone isn't enough; cooperation ensures maximum benefit. But to establish cooperation, you first teach the principles and practices of *teamwork*."

Her words struck deeper than before. I wasn't just hearing them—I was beginning to understand.

Her voice became almost reverent. "And that, Patrick, is the critical key. The ideal environment to instill cooperation is within families. High-functioning families exemplify *teamwork* naturally—it's the foundation of a sustainable society. By studying the elements of cooperation and teaching them to children, you initiate a self-perpetuating virtuous cycle."

She paused, awaiting my reaction. "And their children refine and teach the next generation, who then—"

"Rinse and repeat," I interjected with a smile, finally understanding.

Vanatta smiled kindly, recognizing my metaphor for the self-perpetuating cycle she was describing.

"Okay, how about another example?"

"Suppose" Vanatta presented thoughtfully, "you allow politicians to lie, or even stretch the truth. When your society discovers its leaders aren't required to be truthful, people naturally begin assuming those leaders are lying. Trust disappears."

I sighed deeply. "But that's exactly how it is in my country."

She smiled sympathetically, "Yes, it is." Clearly, she'd chosen this example deliberately. "And hasn't this led to cynicism and disengagement throughout your society?"

"Absolutely," I admitted. "My friends hardly pay any attention to politics. They feel powerless."

"That's social math—another foreseeable cause and effect. When one person lies to another, it violates the supreme value of Equality. The liar claims a privileged position by distorting truth, creating imbalance and mistrust."

Suddenly, a light bulb turned on in my mind. "So, the moment we accept politicians lying, we can already predict people will eventually feel powerless. They disengage because the relationship between leaders and citizens is no longer equal, violating the Equality value."

Vanatta nodded approvingly. "Indeed. And what happens when a critical mass of citizens disengages from self-governance?"

"They lose it," I realized soberly. "Their system becomes unsustainable."

Vanatta nodded before continuing, "Here on Avona, we've long understood that reality. We sanctify Equality because it fosters truthfulness. We hold each other accountable—always. Truth is the backbone of every relationship in our society. Without universally accessible truth, how can we expect citizens to equally realize their highest potential? We have zero tolerance for deception, as it's fundamentally destructive. Social math."

It was undeniably logical. I realized then that social math wasn't just theory—on Avona, it was the very blueprint of their flourishing society. Vanatta gave me space to absorb this concept before she gently offered another illustration.

"Patrick, if I ask you, 'What's two plus two?' do you have to think about it before answering?"

I shook my head. "No, it's automatic. I know the answer before you've finished asking."

"And why is that?"

"I don't know—school, maybe? It's been drilled into my mind, and I've seen it proven countless times."

"Of course you have," she affirmed. "Social math works similarly for us. We know, without question, which behaviors lead to successful outcomes, and which don't, based on centuries of study, education, and consistent, proven results. Our society has no tolerance for deception, because we've repeatedly observed the harm it does. Our focus on parenting as society's most critical responsibility also stems directly from this concept of social math."

Despite grasping her logic, I felt the cultural conditioning from Earth pulling at me. "Honestly, Vanatta, a lot of this sounds like socialism—at least that's what people back home might call it. I'm not sure my country—or my world—is ready for that."

Vanatta smiled knowingly, "We don't call it anything, Patrick—just a functioning government. It truly doesn't matter what ideological label you give it. What matters is integrity. The structure of your government must, above all else, be completely free from corruption."

"Right. You've emphasized that before."

"Indeed," she continued gently. "Any form of governance that rigorously applies the seven supreme values as its standard of measurement, inevitably becomes sustainable. If a society conscientiously follows this path—one step at a time—it naturally arrives at the kind of stability and flourishing you see on Avona."

Vanatta paused thoughtfully, letting me fully grasp the depth of her insights. I swished my feet smoothly just under the surface of the reflecting pond as we sat in comfortable silence. After several minutes, she resumed, thoughtfully expanding on her earlier points.

"Beyond family," she explained, "our highest personal pursuit is philosophy, followed closely by public service. Elected office is limited to just two terms. We have no professional politicians—but also no shortage of capable, ethical citizens eager to serve. On Avona, elected service is regarded as a tremendous honor."

I smiled ruefully, contrasting Avona's attitude with Earth's political reality.

Vanatta sensed my thought. "In a society that prioritizes equality and public service, everyone receives genuine care and support. When the seven supreme values become the ultimate metric—an irreducible standard—institutions naturally become sustainable, and society thrives."

Her expression became more serious.

"But I remind you—none of this can happen until you remove social predators. Predators refuse to follow rules, causing those who do to live in perpetual fear—the primary cause of your world's destructive cycle."

She stopped and faced me, her gaze gentle yet direct. "Simply put, Patrick, that fear is killing you. It poisons every attempt at growth."

She let that sit for a moment, then continued, "Your fear is like acid in the recipe of life—it eats away at progress, goodwill, and trust. Until you rid yourselves of that acid, nothing wholesome can take root."

The words cracked something open inside me. That metaphor—**acid**—hit differently. Not just as a poetic turn of phrase, but as something disturbingly accurate. I could feel it.

In our politics.

In our relationships.

In the way we parent and punish, defend and divide.

Fear was everywhere—eating away at the very things we claimed to be building.

"The irony," she said softly, "is that your fear of death actually contributes to killing you—it sabotages life itself."

I swallowed hard. That line didn't just land—it detonated. Because I'd seen it.

In the way people cling to comfort, defend outdated beliefs, or lash out when they feel threatened. Fear made us irrational. Defensive. Small. And we called it survival.

Vanatta inched closer, her voice a gentle balm.

"It's destroying your people, your ecosystems, even your planet. To escape it, you must deal with the predators who perpetuate it—and give your societies the safety they so desperately need."

I vividly recalled Landorf's analogy—how even one 'rotten apple' spoils the rest. Considering how Avona had systematically eliminated predatory behaviors, their meticulous focus on parenting suddenly made perfect sense—**stop predators before they take root**.

Following my thoughts, Vanatta's voice softened, offering me hope.

"Once you do that, your society will naturally follow the virtuous cycle rooted in the seven supreme values.

"The river of culture flows clean again."

The purity of her message gripped my soul. And for a while, we simply sat there—silent, side by side, our feet swirling softly through the cool water, as if stirring the stillness of my own transformation.

Chapter 14

Conquer Thyself

The water lapped quietly at the stone's edge, echoing the silence we'd shared for what felt like hours. My thoughts remained steeped in everything Vanatta had revealed—hope, responsibility, and the scale of what lay ahead.

She offered me a path forward—but now, as the light of wisdom was dawning, all I could feel was the weight of the journey.

"Is this really possible?" I whispered, barely realizing I'd said it aloud.

I turned to Vanatta and shook my head. "It just feels like too much weight for one person to carry."

She only smiled, as if holding some secret comfort she wasn't quite ready to share. Her calm patience still held me in quiet awe.

"Patrick," she said softly, "let's walk."

Silently, gratefully, I rose and followed her along the winding garden path—one I was beginning to recognize in that strange, *feeling-at-home* kind of way.

We soon arrived at the familiar gazebo where my journey of insights had begun just the day before. Landorf sat comfortably on his stootle in the dappled shade, smiling as though he'd been expecting us.

After a few moments of light conversation, Vanatta excused herself to begin preparations for our evening meal. With a knowing glance and the faintest grin, she handed me off to Landorf like a seasoned guide easing me into the hands of another.

I settled onto the stootle beside him, instantly calmed by the reassuring warmth of his steady gaze. Just his presence seemed to whisper that good things were still possible.

"Fear not," Landorf spoke gently, clearly sensing my lingering doubt. "You have help."

"Help?" I echoed cautiously.

"Yes, Patrick—help. It's always there... for the asking."

I shifted uneasily. "Honestly, I have no idea what you're talking about. But I do know this—Earth will need *all* the help it can get if we're ever going to come close to what Avona has achieved."

"Then listen closely," he leaned in slightly, adding gravitas to what he was about to say.

"When what you ask is wise, unselfish, in service to your growth and the well-being of others—it will *always* be granted."

I hesitated. I was sure he already knew the question forming in my mind, but I asked it anyway, my voice quieter than usual.

"Help from where?"

"Within you dwells a Divine Spark."

I tensed. A flicker of discomfort rose in me instantly. It sounded... religious—and that wasn't something I identified with.

Landorf, ever attuned, waited patiently as I wrestled with it.

"I'm not really religious," I admitted. "I mean, I do sense there's... something—maybe something like your Creator. But organized religion just doesn't resonate with me."

"Nor should it," came his surprising reply. "The Creator isn't moved by rituals, and needs no middleman to hear you. On Avona, we have no formal religions—no rigid doctrines.

"Spirituality, for us, is purely personal, a private relationship with The Creator—unique to each individual."

His words washed over me with refreshing simplicity, a far cry from the preachiness and evangelical fervor I'd grown up hearing back on Earth.

"So, when you say we have help..." I prompted softly, now intrigued.

"When you seek truth from within," Landorf advised, "guided by your Divine Spark... that is *true* religion."

His voice held quiet conviction, eyes steady with warmth. There was no pressure, no sermon. Just a clear invitation to believe in something already mine.

The purity of his words, the gentleness of his presence—it captivated me. I wanted to understand more.

"You can even have celestial guides," he added with a kind smile. "But you must ask. Every mortal—every human—is spiritually endowed with divine riches, though many refuse to believe it.

"You have the power to summon into existence whatever you can imagine... if it aligns with the will of The Creator."

Despite the reassuring warmth in Landorf's eyes, my skepticism clawed at me. "How could something so intangible possibly tackle Earth's vast problems?"

"Patrick, your Divine Spark isn't abstract mysticism—it's the very real, yet quiet voice within that speaks to your intuition, your innate sense of rightness. Trust it, and clarity will always follow."

Despite the beauty of his words, a part of me still resisted. As inspiring as it sounded, some stubborn thread inside me clung to doubt—the quiet belief that real change required more than good intentions and inner whispers.

Landorf sensed it, but didn't push. He simply waited, patient as ever.

"When your requests align with truth, beauty, and goodness," his voice reducing almost to a whisper, "they will be answered—not always immediately, but always at the right time."

He paused again, not for emphasis, but to give space—space for the truth to breathe, to land.

"Listen closely to your inner guide, Patrick. Measure each choice against the seven supreme values. If you stay on that path... certainty will come. So will peace. And the strength of personal conviction."

"But I'm just one person," I protested, my voice thin with doubt. "How could that possibly change anything if no one else walks the same path?"

Landorf inhaled slowly and let out a long breath, his eyes steady and unwavering. "Patrick, you already know this… but, you still resist it: *You can only control you.*"

I nodded, quiet now, sensing something important was coming.

His tone shifted—no longer gentle, but commanding. His gaze locked onto mine with startling intensity.

"The greatest achievement in any mortal life," he said, his voice firm and deliberate, "is to **conquer thyself.**"

The sudden force in his words struck me like a bell. It wasn't anger—it was conviction. The kind that left no room for argument.

"Not riches. Not empires. Not cities or power," he continued, leaning forward. "There is *no* greater triumph than mastering your fears."

He held the moment. Let it burn.

"Conquer thyself."

His words echoed with powerful clarity, reverberating through my consciousness. I sat in silence, absorbing the impact.

"Conquer thyself," he repeated, his voice gentler now. "Lead others solely by example. That's the secret to a victorious life. Measure each decision and action consciously against the supreme values. When they align, you'll know you've stepped onto the paradise path."

The truth landed deep. I realized, maybe for the first time, how futile it was to try to change others. I had no power over them—only over myself. And maybe that was the point all along.

Conquer thyself, I repeated inwardly, letting it settle like a mantra. Again and again it echoed, until it softened into something even truer: *It's not my job to change others—conquer thyself.*

Landorf, ever attuned, offered one final reassurance.

"You were never asked to transform the world, Patrick. Only yourself. And in doing so, you'll lead—without ever needing to command."

Relief washed over me. I wasn't a messiah—just a man with flaws. But improving myself? That was enough. That was everything.

Conquer thyself, I thought again.

Sensing this revelation had penetrated my being, Landorf gently reminded me that, "Every significant societal shift in your planet's history began with a small group—or even a single individual—who chose to embody the values they believed in, eventually influencing others until a critical mass was reached."

Then, as if reading my soul, he concluded softly, "And one day, as more of your people live by this quiet truth—one person at a time—a tipping point will come. As enough individuals choose to evolve, your civilization will change—and eventually your world will become settled in its own era of *Light and Life*.

"It begins with the belief that it's possible—and the willingness to follow the leadings of your own Divine Spark."

"As we sat quietly in the placidity of the late afternoon, I felt lighter, as if a burden had lifted—but I knew my journey wasn't over yet.

Chapter 15

A Settled Universe

Beneath the gazebo in the gentle warmth of the fading afternoon, our conversation had eased into peaceful, contemplative silence. The Avonian sky began to deepen, promising another spectacular display of breathtaking sunset colors.

Yet, even in this peaceful moment, one persistent question kept surfacing in my mind—quietly nagging me ever since arriving on Avona:

Why?

Why would Deja care so deeply about Earth's fate? Why would Landorf and Vanatta dedicate so much time and energy—so much genuine care—to guiding me patiently through the complex maze of Earth's challenges?

Maybe they were simply incredibly kind beings? Honestly, that wouldn't surprise me at all. Yet, deep down, I couldn't silence my curiosity. On my planet, genuine altruism felt rare; most people seemed driven by self-interest. Was there something more?

The question kept nagging me with growing intensity. I had to know—*what was in it for them?*

Gently, I broke our silence.

"Landorf," I began softly, feeling slightly awkward as I gathered my thoughts, "there's something I've wanted to ask you ever since Deja brought me here—just out of curiosity, really. I hope it doesn't sound ungrateful or suspicious—that's definitely not my intention."

He glanced warmly toward me, his calm eyes encouraging. "Go ahead, Patrick. You can always ask any question that comes to mind."

Of course, I knew he knew what I was thinking, and that gave me some degree of comfort.

"Alright, well…" I began hesitantly, trying to phrase my question graciously. "I don't mean this badly—but why exactly do you and Vanatta—and Deja—care so deeply about what happens to Earth? Is there… uh, something else behind all of this?"

A radiant smile spread slowly across Landorf's face. He seemed pleased I'd finally asked. Suddenly, it felt as though I was about to discover something profoundly important.

"Patrick," he said thoughtfully, eyes glowing with quiet approval, "I appreciate your question more than you know. It means you're ready to understand the larger picture."

I leaned forward, immediately intrigued, silently eager to hear whatever secret he was about to reveal.

"Earth and Avona," he began slowly, with great gravitas, "are not isolated, independent worlds. Far from it. Our planets belong to a greater family of evolutionary worlds, each connected in a shared cosmic destiny."

My heart quickened with fascination.

He continued, almost solemnly "Every evolutionary world begins its journey in primitive conditions. Over countless millennia, they advance through stages of biological, social, and spiritual development until they reach a perfected state of peace, stability, and fulfillment— what we call being *settled* in Light and Life."

I nodded thoughtfully. "And Avona is already there, right?"

"Yes," Landorf affirmed softly. "But we are only one world. Within our local system—our immediate cosmic neighborhood—there are exactly one thousand inhabited planets, each uniquely progressing toward that same goal. Some, like Avona, have already arrived. Others are still on the journey."

I paused, heart sinking slightly. "And Earth…? Where are we in that picture?"

He took a long breath, his expression serious yet compassionate. "Unfortunately, Patrick, your world is not merely lagging behind—it's teetering dangerously close to regression."

I swallowed hard, the words confirming my deepest fears. "What exactly does that mean?"

"It means Earth risks losing the precious progress it has made. Rather than moving toward stability and enlightenment, your world is poised on the edge of a profound spiritual and social setback."

I sat back, stunned. Somehow, I'd feared this—but hearing it spoken aloud made it real. *We weren't just stuck—we were slipping.* His words hung heavily in the air. Quietly, he gave me a moment to absorb them before continuing—his voice now both urgent and hopeful.

"But Patrick, there's something even greater at stake. The true purpose of planetary evolution isn't just the settlement of individual worlds—it's something far more grand."

His eyes sparkled with quiet excitement. "The ultimate objective—the universe's highest destiny—is the settlement, not just of individual planets, but entire planetary systems, then sectors, and eventually, the entire local universe itself, into Light and Life."

My voice came out barely above a whisper as I grasped his meaning. "A perfected universe?"

"Yes," he affirmed gently. "But understand this clearly: universal perfection cannot occur until every single inhabited world reaches its own settled status. Until Earth is settled in Light, our local planetary family remains incomplete—unable to fully cross into perfected peace and harmony."

The enormity of this truth stunned me. "So, what happens on Earth… affects not just us, but you too?"

Landorf nodded slightly. "In ways you have yet to imagine. Your world's struggles, its triumphs or failures—they ripple across this universe sector. When Earth moves forward, Patrick, its advancement lifts the entire planetary family—bringing all of us closer to our universal destiny.

He gazed upward briefly, eyes shining as if reflecting the stars.

"Your planet's future matters—not just to you, but to all of us. If Earth regresses, it may take millennia to regain its current spiritual and cultural achievements. It would delay our entire local universe's advancement toward universal harmony."

He paused, allowing me to grasp the gravity of his words. My heart felt simultaneously crushed beneath the immense weight of responsibility and buoyed by a profound sense of meaning. Never had I felt so insignificant yet undeniably essential at the same time.

"So now Patrick, you understand. This is a shared destiny—a cosmic collaboration, intricately woven into the very fabric of the universe itself."

I sat back slowly, deeply humbled and profoundly moved. "And when every planet, including Earth, eventually settles into Light and Life… what then?"

A radiant smile returned to Landorf's face. "Then, Patrick, our local universe becomes settled in Light and Life—fully aligned with divine wisdom, truth, beauty, and goodness. A perfected state. Universal harmony **by freewill choice**—the fulfillment of The Creator's plan, and readiness to move forward into the next unrevealed stage of universe evolution."

I sat in stunned silence for over a minute. My mind was blown! The immensity of what he revealed so greatly exceeded anything I could ever even dream of.

Then he added, "That is the vision we hold. It's why Avona is so deeply invested in Earth's success. Your destiny and ours are inseparable. Your world's progress lifts us all."

In that moment, something shifted deep within me. For the first time, I felt how deeply Earth mattered—not just to humanity, but in a cosmic sense I had never imagined.

"I understand now," I said softly. "We really are all connected, aren't we?"

Landorf smiled gently, nodding. "Yes we are, Patrick. We are *all* connected."

For several long minutes, silence settled over us. My gaze drifted slowly around the peaceful courtyard—the jade-like pillars, the 'edible' mosaic pathways, the softly burbling fountain, vividly colorful birds darting gracefully among the lush foliage. The garden's sweet fragrances and the serene beauty of Avona seemed to echo his hopeful message.

Landorf gave me space to absorb the enormity of our discussion, saying nothing as the silence did its work. Eventually, as the weight of his words settled comfortably into my consciousness, he reached over and gently tapped my knee—a friendly gesture, pulling me from cosmic contemplation back to the immediate moment.

"Come," he invited warmly. "Vanatta has prepared a wonderful evening meal. Let's join her and enjoy."

As I stood, following him toward the welcoming glow of the dining hall, I felt something new rising within—a quiet determination to honor the trust placed in me.

I no longer wondered why they cared so deeply. Now, I shared their vision—feeling it resonate deeply within my soul.

Chapter 16

The Soul Purpose

After a meal of impossibly rich fruits, roasted grains, and delicately seasoned nuts—flavors so vibrant they felt almost sacred—we turned to face the Avonian sunset. The sky was ablaze, streaked with surreal shades of violet, amber, and crimson that no earthly palette could replicate.

As silence wrapped around us like a silk veil, Vanatta spoke at last, her voice low and reverent. What she shared next was no ordinary insight—it was her final gift to me: a truth both solemn and luminous, revealing the ultimate purpose of mortal existence.

"Your world, like all evolutionary worlds," she explained softly, "is an incubator for souls. Your society's highest duty is to provide every soul the chance to thrive—beginning with a sound body and a steady mind. A soul experiencing life through a struggling body or a challenged mind faces greater difficulties connecting with the Divine Spark that indwells all minds capable of moral choosing and spiritual yearning.

"The more robust and stable your average citizen becomes, the greater the possibility for developing richly weighted souls, filled with worthwhile experiences. In turn, such evolved souls naturally uplift their societies, creating a virtuous cycle that moves ever closer to *settled status*—like what you see here on Avona.

"Your world is a cocoon—temporary, fragile, but essential. It exists to help you grow a soul of substantial experience, wisdom, strong character, patience, compassion, empathy, and love for humanity. These virtues are within reach of every normal mortal.

"Remember," she emphasized, "the universe is one vast, endless school—a place of continuous learning and infinite growth. **Your soul, your truest possession, is the legacy you take with you into eternity.**"

Her words lingered like incense in a sacred hall—delicate, fragrant, and impossible to forget. I was stilled, not just in body but in spirit, my heart full and hushed. I had no words left to offer.

Lost in quiet reflection, I excused myself and slipped away to my room—unsure if I needed sleep, or simply space to hold the immensity of it all.

✳✳✳

I don't recall drifting off, but an angel appeared in my dream, speaking softly yet with clarity:

Life's uncertainties and struggles align precisely with The Creator's plan," she explained. *Courage emerges by facing hardships; strength of character is built by confronting disappointments.*

Without social inequity, altruism would never emerge. Without uncertainty, you would never discover trust or hope. Faith requires not knowing all answers. Love of truth flourishes only where falsehood is possible. Idealism surfaces amid relative beauty and goodness.

Loyalty and devotion thrive precisely because betrayal exists. Unselfishness develops only by overcoming your desire for recognition. True pleasure is fully appreciated only against the presence of pain and suffering.

The Creator, in infinite wisdom, endowed you with experiences that cultivate these essential virtues. Although you may not fully comprehend this wisdom in this lifetime, your understanding and gratitude will blossom as you progress spiritually toward Paradise.

And then she slowly faded away, as softly as she had appeared.

It was a restful, satisfying sleep—as though some deeper part of me had embraced my soul-purpose in life, knowing a glorious planetary destiny was waiting patiently to unfold.

When I awoke, bright morning sunlight leaked through the cracks in the wall of my Napoʻopoʻo beach shack. For a long moment, I lay utterly still, the dream's profound truths lingering vividly in my mind. The familiar sounds of the nearby surf and the salty smell of sea breeze gently pulled me back into earthly reality. *Had it all been a dream?*

Seconds later, my 7AM radio alarm clicked on. The morning DJ sang out…

♫ *It's Aloha Friday, no work till Monday…* ♫

—and just like that, I remembered: *I was scheduled to work.*

I jumped up in a daze, suspended somewhere between two worlds. I showered, ate, and then went to grab my mask and fins.

All I saw was the empty hook. They were gone.

And I never did find them.

Over 40 Years Later...

The clarity of every conversation remains vivid—undimmed, un-shakable, complete.

I've done my best to live those truths; To conquer myself, as Landorf had urged… to grow my soul as Vanatta so graciously encouraged… and through it all, to follow the whispering wisdom of my own Divine Spark.

I've measured each decision against the seven supreme values—perhaps not perfectly, but always with intention. And always with heart.

And today, as I ride this tiny blue dot for my seventy-third trip around our nearest star, I realize—*I can't leave this world without telling this story.*

To stay silent would feel like a betrayal of everything I was shown.

So, today I opened my notebook and began...

Peering through my mask, floating face down on the glass-calm waters of Kealakekua Bay, I barely noticed the soft whistle of my breath through the snorkel as the late-morning Hawaiian sun gently warmed my back. Twenty feet below ...

The End

STEFFEN PATRICK   *The author, 1981*

From the Author

Truth belongs to everyone. Wisdom is never truly ours alone. It rises from the long stream of voices and insights of those who came before us, and it flows from a Source far greater still. At best, we discover a spark, refine it, and carry it forward.

These pages hold truths I've stumbled upon, glimpsed, and been compelled to share. They don't belong to me. They belong to all who are ready to hear, and to those who will carry them forward.

May you welcome them with an open mind, hold them in an open heart, and carry them forward with wisdom.

Steffen Patrick